"How can you doubt me?

"I called your home and left messages for you to call me. I did *everything* I could to make sure you got that property," she said.

Tears glistened in Carly's eyes as she turned, almost falling. Strong arms reached for her and held her close. "Never speak to me again, Mr. Noble. Never!"

"Never is such a long time, Carly. Is that what you want? Or is it this?"

As he brought his mouth to hers and kissed her, all she wanted was to surrender to his passion. But Adam gently stepped away. "I want to believe you, Carly. But I can't."

AVAILABLE FROM FERN MICHAELS

GOLDEN LASSO

Derek Bannon would win Jan Warren's ranch—at any cost. Yet as his ambition slowly destroyed her, his touch brought her senses alive. Because there was one thing Derek wanted more than her ranch. He wanted Jan....

BEYOND TOMORROW

Adam Noble was looking for a home. And his millions could get him any house he wanted. All he needed now was Carly Andrews to make his life complete. But what would it take to make the elusive Carly his wife?

PAINT ME RAINBOWS

Jilted at the altar, Jill Barton was running from love. But when handsome Logan Matthews offered her sanctuary, she was far from safe. Logan stirred up desires she'd never felt before. And his passion left her nowhere to run....

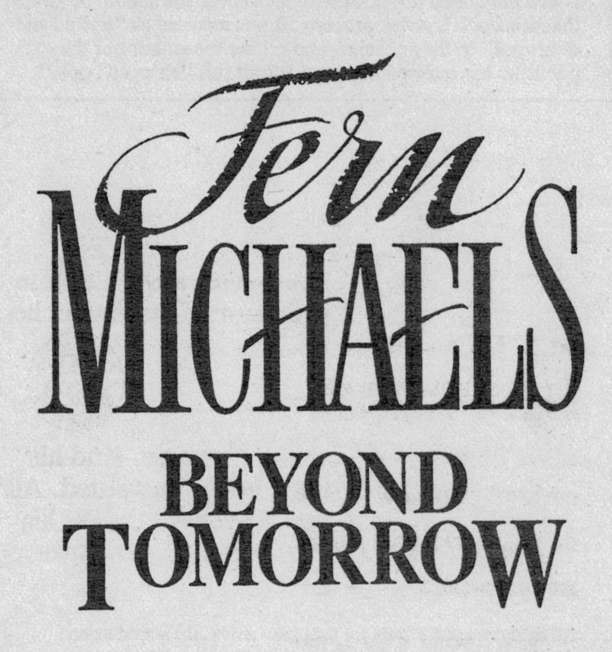

Silhouette® Books

Published by Silhouette Books
America's Publisher of Contemporary Romance

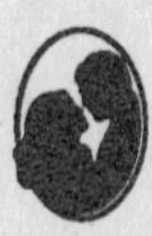
SILHOUETTE BOOKS

BEYOND TOMORROW

ISBN 0-373-48302-3

This edition published by arrangement with Harlequin Enterprises B. V.

Printed in U.S.A.

Available from Fern Michaels

Golden Lasso
Beyond Tomorrow
Paint Me Rainbows

Chapter One

A slate gray evening sky accompanied by intermittent drizzles of a chill rain was characteristic of a bright July summer day in the resort community of Bar Harbor, Maine. The unrelenting drops fell into skips of puddles and flooded the gutters outside the low, one-story building at the far end of Main Street, staining the cedar shingles a muddy brown. It was nearing eight o'clock, a time when most of the businesses in town had closed for the day, but several lamps glowed from within, illuminating the mullioned windows and falling on the neatly lettered sign signifying "Andrews Realty."

Carly Andrews worked diligently at her desk, her soft, dark hair cloaking her delicate, patrician profile as she bent her head. The papers fluttered beneath her gracefully long fingers as she studied them, and they softly reflected the color of her azure-blue silk blouse. Long legs, clad in white linen slacks, crossed and uncrossed beneath the desk, and her shoeless feet habitually rubbed into the soft yellow pile carpeting. The entire office was tastefully furnished in muted pastel colors with bric-a-brac placed casually, but deliberately, on gleaming end tables. The whole effect was feminine and frilly, and Carly had often complained to her mother, whose taste the office reflected, that it was more like an eighteenth century boudoir than an efficient realty agency.

"It's a steal! A steal!" cried a raucous, ear-piercing voice. "No points! Mortgage!" the crackly voice continued to shout.

Carly cast a baleful eye in the parrot's direction and continued with her work. The parrot fluttered his green plumage and then tucked one foot under his wing.

"Quincy, go to sleep," Carly muttered in the bird's direction as she tilted the directoire lamp for better light. Lord, was she tired. What she didn't need right now was a talkative parrot.

"Darling, are you still at it? Tomorrow is another day. It's time we both went home and had some dinner. I'm sure the James couple will take the property." The elegant, pencil-slim woman patted her silver hair and pretended to scold. "All work and no play makes Jack a dull boy. We don't want that to happen to our Carly, do we, Quincy?" she cajoled the bird who was older than Methuselah and had been handed down through three generations of the Andrews family. There were times that Carly believed Quincy knew more secrets about the Andrews family and had more solid business sense locked up in his feathery little head than she would ever learn in a lifetime.

Carly put down her pencil and slumped in her high-backed chair. Her voice was patient when she spoke, as though she had had long years of practice, but it was also respectful and loving. "Mother, between you and Quincy I can't get anything done. First of all, I am not dull. Second, I had lunch at three-thirty and I'm not hungry right now. Third, I want to finish this contract this evening because I have a breakfast date with the Hollisters in the morning. I gave my word I'd have it ready for them. Why don't you go home? You've had a long day too and I know you're tired. And take this creature with you." She pointed her finger at the perch where Quincy spent most business days.

Melissa Andrews looked down at her daughter, a frown creasing her porcelain doll features. Her voice was slightly petulant when she replied, "Are you saying I have to eat alone? Sometimes, Carly, I think you do this deliberately."

Immediately, Carly was apologetic. Sometimes, she thought, things got to be too much for her and she became testy. Her tone softened.

"All right, if you insist on being maternal this evening, you can stop at the deli and get me a pastrami sandwich. I'll have it when I get home which should be within the hour."

Melissa placed her hands on her slim hips and clucked her tongue. "The deli is out of my way, darling. How about peanut butter and jelly? And a can of clam chowder? I declare, I positively envy your appetite and it never shows on your figure."

"Fine, Mother, peanut butter and jelly will be just fine. Skip the chowder. Don't forget to take Quincy with you. I'll be along soon."

"Carly, I can't take Quincy. He messes my upholstery. And," she added indignantly, "he flutters his wings when I stop for a light. People think I'm positively strange. You bring him with you," she directed, closing the front door behind her.

"Life is hell! War is hell! Squawk!" Quincy babbled to Melissa's departure.

"Now that you've almost exhausted your vocabulary, bird, why don't you go to sleep?" Carly snapped, throwing a cover over the bird's cage.

Ah, peace and quiet for a little while at least. She sighed deeply and propped her slim ankles on an open desk drawer. She leaned back in her chair and let her eyes scan the pages in front of her. All she really had to do was make a final check on her figures with the calculator and she could call it a night. Satisfied with the contract, Carly slid the pages into a folder and then stuffed it into her tote bag. Looking around the office, she had the feeling she was forgetting something. She shrugged. If she was, it would be a simple matter of returning to the office first thing in the morning before having breakfast with her clients. She knew she had done a fine job and the commission was going to be healthy. Time to go home to that peanut butter and jelly on toast.

Removing the throw from the bird's cage, she waited for the parrot to emerge and settle himself on her shoulder. Carly laughed as she bent beneath the desk to find her high-heeled sandals. She was laughing aloud at Quincy's antics as he nipped playfully and tickled her neck and ear. She emerged from her very unladylike position with her shoes in her hand in time to see a tall, muscular man and a high-cheekboned woman with an incredibly willowy figure enter her office. Carly blushed a brilliant crimson and moistened her dry lips. Quincy continued with his nudging and nipping.

The man's voice was brisk and cool, heavy with authority, but holding a warm note of graciousness. "Miss Andrews, I'm Adam Noble, and this is Simone Maddox."

The woman was stylishly dressed and perfectly coiffed, and succeeded in exuding poise and control from the tips of her scarlet painted fingers to the soles of her needle thin heeled shoes. From the looks of her finely arched brows and the slight, disdainful curl of her lip, it was evident that *she* would never be caught with her posterior in the air, groping beneath the furniture for her shoes. *And* with a shrill-mouthed bird flapping on her shoulder!

Carly nodded to acknowledge the introduction.

"I realize this is after business hours, but the door was open and your lights are on."

Simone Maddox pulled on Adam Noble's arm, "Don't be silly, Adam. No one in his right mind would turn away from a chance to do business with any of *the* Nobles." Her sharp glance rested on Carly, defying her to deny it.

Carly's jaw tightened. "You're correct, Mr. Noble, it is after business hours." They were all alike—the idle rich who came to Bar Harbor, Maine, to spend their summers while they waited expectantly for the new social season to open in the fall. Then they would flock to New York or London or Paris like mindless geese following an ancient migration route. But it was their haughty contempt of the Bar Harbor locals that so annoyed Carly. True, the little town did exist on the "summer people" trade and tourism, but it rankled her that they would take it for granted that she would stay after hours and then fall down on her knees just to serve one of the celebrated Nobles. "I'll be glad to discuss whatever it is you would like tomorrow during business hours. Shall I make an appointment for you?" Carly's abrupt tone was not lost on the ravishing woman at Adam Noble's side.

"But, darling, you're just standing there with that...that...creature on your shoulder and holding your shoes. We really only want a few minutes of your time." While Simone Maddox's voice implored Carly to reconsider, her attitude made it clear she was unused to being denied.

"You've already had a few minutes of my time, and I'm late for an appointment. As I said, if you care to come back tomorrow, I'll make an appointment with you now. At that time you will have my undivided attention." Why was she behaving this way? Normally she wasn't rude. And why was her stomach churning like a windmill?

Adam Noble had the bluest eyes she had ever seen and they were staring right through her. From the look he was giving her, this must be some kind of first for him. People in Bar Harbor catered to the Nobles who accepted it as their due. Well, Carly Andrews didn't bow and scrape—to the Nobles or anyone else for that matter. It was clear Adam Noble didn't care for her abrupt rebuff, and it wasn't sitting well.

"My apologies, Miss Andrews. I just wanted to ask you about some property. If you aren't interested, I can go somewhere else."

"Life is hell! War is hell!" shouted Quincy as he left Carly's shoulder and circled the room in a feather flap of wings and finally perched on the desk.

Carly bristled. "Perhaps you didn't hear me, Mr. Noble. I said I would be glad to discuss business with you tomorrow. If that doesn't interest you, then there's little I can do about it." Two rebuffs in one night. In the short span of a few minutes! Probably a new experience for him.

"She's not interested," Miss Maddox cooed. "Come, darling, we'll go to another agency. A place where people know the value of handling business for the Nobles."

An angry surge of adrenaline shot through Carly. It always came down to power and money. Walk softly and carry a big stick. Money was always the club. "Let's go, Quincy, time to go home." The parrot flew to her shoulder and settled himself.

"Miss Maddox, try Olsen Realty on Main Street. Mr. Olsen runs a very efficient business, when he's not out fishing. Now, if you'll excuse me, I really do have to leave."

Adam Noble moved almost imperceptibly so that he was standing directly in front of Carly. "My apologies, Miss Andrews, for assuming I didn't need an appointment. I'll call tomorrow, and perhaps we can set something up. And, Miss Andrews, don't you think you should put your shoes on? It's raining outside." He grinned, showing perfect white teeth. Miss Maddox giggled. Carly froze in her tracks.

"Good night to both of you," she managed to choke out. Adam Noble was staring at her and his blue gaze seemed to see much more, which made Carly uncomfortable.

To cover her confusion, Carly reached for Quincy and held him as the couple exited the office. Quickly, Carly lowered the shade on the front door and then locked it securely. She turned off the lights and left by the back door, her shoes still in her hand. The shock of the cold rain puddles made her gasp. It was a good thing her mother hadn't been around or she would be hearing about this for the next twenty years. Melissa Andrews' biggest moment in life would be to sell something to the Noble clan. Her mother had been wrong. Tonight, she had been anything but dull. Actually, she frowned, she had been downright obnoxious. She wasn't *that* tired. Would he come back to the office, and if he did, would Simone Maddox be with him? Adam Noble had a reputation for escorting elegant women and this one certainly was elegant.

The Andrews' Cape Cod house looked warm and inviting after the chilly rain. The only thing Carly dreaded was her mother's habit of playing twenty questions when she arrived home. If she pretended to be tired, she just might be able to eat her sandwich and retire. She should be so lucky, she mused.

"Mummy dear, you look so ravishing," Carly laughed as she eyed the tissue wrapped hair and her mother's shiny face. "If your clients could see you now, what would they say?"

"They would say that I'm an indulgent mother. Look, I even put some pickles on your plate. Eat, before it gets cold."

"Mother, a peanut butter and jelly sandwich can't get cold and pickles come from the refrigerator. If that's the best you can do with your mothering, retire. Besides, I've been thinking, since we both hate housework and cooking, why don't we hire someone to come in for a few days a week? The agency is making enough money."

"I won't hear of it. I detest people prying and poking into my things. You wouldn't like it either, Carly. The answer is no. If you would find yourself a beau, you could dine out more often. Just look at you, Carly," Melissa said, forging ahead on her favorite subject. "You're as pretty as a picture, smart as a whip, you have a college degree, and you don't even have a boyfriend, much less a steady. You're twenty-three, Carly. Time is moving on and you know what they say about late starters."

"Can't you see that I'm a late bloomer, Mother? I like my life the way it is. When and if the right man comes along, I'll know it. You don't want to become an interfering mother-in-law or a grandmother before your time. That's a fate worse than death, right?"

"I don't expect you to jump into anything, but for heaven's sake, Carly, you could at least get your feet wet."

"I did, Mother, I did." Carly said, at Melissa's puzzled look, as she thought of how she had gone barefoot in the rain puddles. "Never mind, it was a sort of joke."

"You're the prettiest girl in town and you know it. Just the other day Judge Noble was telling me he saw you out on the interstate, and he couldn't believe his eyes."

"The reason he couldn't believe his eyes was because I was changing a flat tire. He had his chauffeur stop to offer help but I was all finished."

"Well, he said you were the prettiest girl in town and those are his exact words. He also said he hoped Adam would look you up one of these days. The judge doesn't seem to care for the flashy women Adam has been squiring around. Adam is the catch of the season. And another thing,"

Melissa said, lowering her voice to a hushed whisper, "there's talk that Adam is going to run for the Senate. Aren't you going to say something?" Melissa demanded, annoyed at Carly's lack of enthusiasm.

"I'm sorry that the Noble clan doesn't interest me as much as they do you, Mother. As far as I can see, all they do is throw their weight around and pretend they own the whole town. Adam and his brother Cayce are playboys, and the girls sit in the beauty shop and the spa all day. If you think that's a worthwhile life, then you're welcome to it. Society, Mother, is not all it's made out to be," Carly said tartly. She carried her plate to the sink and rinsed it. "I'm going to take a shower now and turn in. I have an early breakfast appointment. Good night, Mother." Instantly contrite over her tart tone to her mother, Carly turned and wrapped her arms around the slim woman. "Mom, you just have to stop trying to match me up with one of the rich men who vacation here. I'll find my own man when I'm ready. I'm happy, really I am. I know how you love the social set around here, and that's just fine for you. It's not fine for me."

"Oh, Carly, you haven't called me Mom since you were little. All right, all right, you live your life and I'll live mine. I'll cook Sunday dinner, how's that?''

"Fine, Mom. Now, let's hit the sack. We both have a busy day tomorrow."

"You go along, I'll lock up and turn off the lights," Melissa Andrews said with a hint of a tear in her eye. "Good night, Carly."

Chapter Two

It was three o'clock according to Carly's watch, and still Adam Noble hadn't made his promised call. Surely, he wouldn't just pop in again without an appointment, not after last night. Another half hour and they would close the agency until Monday morning. He had exactly thirty minutes to make his presence known, preferably without the seductive Simone Maddox in tow.

Carly turned back to her paperwork and the next time she looked at the square digital watch on her wrist, it read 3:58. The phone shrilled on her desk. Sighing, Carly picked it up. "Andrews Realty, may I help you?"

"Miss Andrews, this is Adam Noble." Carly swallowed and patted at her stomach to quiet the swarming butterflies. "I would like to make an appointment for the early part of next week. I'm here on vacation, so my time is my own. Make the appointment at your convenience."

"Just a moment, Mr. Noble, and let me see when I'm free." Carly held the phone away from her ear and shuffled papers on her desk. She knew exactly what her schedule was for the next ten days. "Mr. Noble, I'm free Tuesday morning at eleven-thirty. Is that convenient for you?" Now, why had she said Tuesday instead of Monday? Monday was always a lost day in the real estate business. Nobody ever did anything on Mondays. Even Mr. Olsen didn't do business on Monday. Well, she was stuck with it now.

"Tuesday is fine with me. Would you care to have lunch with me?"

"Lunch would be fine, Mr. Noble." Why not? He probably plans to take it off his income tax, she thought snidely.

"Tuesday it is then. I'll pick you up at the office. Goodbye, Miss Andrews."

"Goodbye, Mr. Noble." They certainly were being polite with each other. She should take Quincy along just to aggravate him. Quincy would straighten him out in three seconds flat. What was wrong with her? Why did she feel she had to come out on top, to get the last word?

Why did she resent him so much? His whole family, for that matter. So, he was born with a silver spoon in his mouth. So what if he went to the best prep schools and the top-notch ivy league colleges? So what if he was tall and handsome? So what if she was jealous of all the slinky Simone Maddoxes? Did he ever work a day in his life? Did he ever do anything but drive a high-powered sports car and sail in one regatta after another, and when he was bored with that, jet off to Monte Carlo and the Riviera? Did she care? No way. The life of the idle rich would not play a part in her life. There was more to life than just breathing.

"Who was that on the phone, Carly?" Melissa asked as she prepared to lock up for the weekend.

"I made an appointment for Tuesday with a prospective client." No point in getting her mother all riled up. She planned to keep the name of her "new client" to herself for as long as possible. If she knew her mother, she would have Carly at the altar within three months, if not sooner.

The weekend passed in a blur. Carly played mixed doubles Saturday and dined at the club with a group of school friends, and on Sunday she brunched with one of her new clients who insisted they wanted to show their appreciation for the fine house Carly had found for them. Monday was maddeningly idle.

Tuesday morning dawned clear and bright as Carly made her way to the office. At the last minute she stopped at the Cottage Inn for a light breakfast. Normally, she just had orange juice and coffee, but today, she felt the need for something a little more substantial. She decided on a poached egg and an apricot danish.

As she drank her coffee, she took special pains not to slosh on her carefully selected outfit. She couldn't go to lunch with her "new client" with coffee and egg stains on her lilac shirt and beige skirt. The pastel of the lilac brought out the hidden blue lights in her ebony hair and did flattering things to her peaches-and-cream complexion. The traffic policeman at the intersection near the wharf had bestowed her an approving smile, and Carly knew she looked fresh and pretty. The day promised to be another hot one with the temperature reaching the high eighties, and with this prospect in mind, she had pulled her hair on top of her head and tied it with a bit of ribbon. A few stray curls escaped to frame her face and trim her long, graceful neck, enhancing her very feminine appearance.

Restlessly, she placed her coffee cup on its saucer and reached for her cotton crocheted handbag to pay her bill. Carly was ashamed of her rude and abrupt behavior toward Adam Noble and at lunch today she knew she must face up to it. In every sense of the word she knew that this was going to be a very long morning.

Somehow, Carly managed to fill in the time after breakfast by shuffling papers from one spot to the other. Melissa, sensing that all was not quite right in her daughter's life, tactfully said she was leaving the office to attend a political luncheon. Carly heaved a sigh of relief when she saw her mother's car leave the lot in back of the agency. Twice she yelled at Quincy who was babbling to himself because of neglect.

"You'd think this was a date or something," Carly muttered to the now sulky parrot. "I wonder if I look all right, not that he's going to notice." Carly frowned. She wondered what Adam Noble thought about freckles. The smattering across the bridge of her nose always bothered her. He probably wouldn't even notice.

A last quick look in her compact mirror and she was ready for anything and everything.

He was prompt; she had to give him that. He had appeared wearing finely tailored white slacks and an open necked shirt beneath a featherweight nautical blazer. A familiar style of dress for most of the Bar Harbor gentlemen who were lunching in town. In the evening most of the clubs demanded more formal dress.

"I thought we would go to the Whale and Porpoise if that's all right with you, Miss Andrews."

"That's fine with me," Carly volunteered.

Adam Noble held the door of the low-slung Mercedes sports coupe open for her. Carly jackknifed herself into the bucket seat and was surprised at the leg room the small car offered. Adam backed the car from the parking slot and drove effortlessly. He was a powerful man, almost as powerful as the car he was driving. Carly liked the fact that he was making small talk and so far had made no mention of the first meeting. If he was willing to start with a clean slate, then she could do the same. She had to admit that he was an impressive man. If only he wasn't such a playboy she might respect him more. Why couldn't he be doing something to earn a living? Such a waste. And where was the ravishing Simone? If only she could ask. But she would bite her tongue off before she did that.

"Here we are," Adam said, maneuvering the little car between two oversized sedans.

He was the perfect escort. He held open the door for her and helped her from the car, and then he held the door of the club open and bowed elaborately, a wide grin splitting his features. Carly grinned and curtsied.

The interior of the Whale and Porpoise was nautical from the entrance foyer to the back room with its fish nets and whaling hooks. The heavy round tables were bare except for place mats. A waitress deftly skirted the tables, holding a tray full of beer steins above her head. Carly liked the jaunty sailor caps the waitresses wore and the bell bottom trousers looked authentic.

Adam held her chair and immediately ordered beer, the Whale and Porpoise's only concession to liquid refreshment. The dark, German beer was just what Carly needed for her parched throat. She found herself admiring the way the heavy mug looked in Adam's strong, sun-bronzed hand. "I love this beer," Carly blurted suddenly.

"I do, too. Sometimes, I drop in here just for a drink. I've had beer the world over and this is by far the best. Unfortunately I have an appointment later on in the day, so I better get down to business. If you don't have any objection to talking while we eat."

"It's all right with me, Mr. Noble. Tell me what I can do for you," Carly said, drawing a small notebook and pen from her bag.

Adam Noble stared at her for a full minute before he replied and then it seemed to Carly he was unsure of what to say or else he changed his mind at the last second and was groping for a new thought. "If we're going to do business together, call me Adam. I believe your name is Carly."

Carly nodded.

"I'm interested in a home for myself. Something within a thirty mile radius of Bar Harbor."

"Mr. . . Adam, you have to start off by changing your wording a little. What you're looking for is a house. Only you can make it a home. Do you understand what I'm saying?"

"Perfectly." There was that strange expression on his face again, and his eyes were so dark, so deep, she felt she could drown in their depths. "I'm looking for a house. I would like a tennis court and a pool, if possible. If the property has neither, I'll still be interested if there's a possibility that I can have both a pool and court built. A fireplace is an absolute necessity. I want one in the family room and one in the master bedroom. I'll require plenty of closet space and a modern kitchen with every gadget that's ever been made. I like to cook."

"Do you really like to cook?" Carly asked in surprise.

"I enjoy it immensely. I'll tell you a secret if you promise never to tell. Did you ever hear of a restaurant in New York called Chez Martine?"

"I've heard of it, but I'm afraid that it's a little too expensive for me. I've heard that the food is magnificent, especially on the weekends."

Adam Noble's eyes danced. "That's because I'm the chef on the weekends. An old college buddy from Brooklyn owns the restaurant and I do private parties for him. Since I've closed my law office I find myself with extra time on my hands and I'm spending more and more of it at Chez Martine."

"That's wonderful!" Carly said exuberantly. "I'll save my money, and perhaps by the end of the summer, I'll be able to afford to dine in your restaurant."

"You'll have to let me know ahead of time so I can prepare something really special. I'll outdo myself," he said proudly. "Now, tell me, is there anything on the market that you think I might be interested in?"

"Offhand, several pieces of property come to mind. How many bedrooms and baths do you want? A one-car garage or two? Are you interested in buying furnishings or do you intend to decorate yourself?"

"At least four bedrooms. I plan to have a lot of kids someday. Same thing with the bathrooms. I'll have the place decorated myself. If it's a deal where the furnishings go with the house or it's a no sale, then I'll buy them. Two- or three-car garage. I have a lot of junk that I've managed to accumulate over the years."

Carly filled her page with scribbles and looked at Adam. "Why don't you just build the kind of house you want?"

"It wouldn't be the same. I want an old house that has seen life. I want old timber, not new green wood. I don't care for chrome and glass and aluminum siding. I want character and white birch trees. Hundreds of them. I want a lawn that has to be mowed, not manicured with a pair of scissors. I want leaves in the fall and buds in the spring. I need a space for a garden so I can grow my herbs. I have some now in small planters, but again, it's not the same. When can you let me know what's on the market?"

"How about tomorrow?"

"That's great, Carly."

"When would you want to move in, assuming that I have something that fits your needs?"

Adam's features closed and his lips tightened. "I'm not sure. You can handle the sale, and whatever time the closing is scheduled for is all right with me. I'm sorry I can't be more definite right now."

"How did you want to finance the property? How much do you want to put down and what's your price range?"

"If you find the right piece of property, money is no object. There's no need for financing. I'll be paying cash. Whatever you need for a deposit will be all right with me."

Carly grimaced. The comfort of money. "You are a most agreeable client, Adam."

Adam grinned. "I do try to please. I'm afraid we got off to a bad start the other night. I was sort of hoping you'd agree to have dinner with me this weekend. To make amends," he added hastily as he saw her hesitate.

"I'd like that, Adam."

"Fine, I'll pick you up Saturday night at seven. Now that our business seems to be taken care of, what do you say we enjoy our lunch and get to know one another? I think I'd like to know you better, Carly Andrews."

And I think I would like to know you better, Adam Noble, Carly said to herself. She smiled and speared a succulent shrimp. This was definitely one of her better days.

Chapter Three

Carly worked industriously the rest of the day poring over new listings. From there she delved into a list of properties she had been compiling over the past two years of possibilities. Possibilities which required a personal call to the homeowner on her part. This was the one part of real estate that she hated. Knocking on strange doors, asking people if they wanted to sell their houses, was not something she enjoyed. For some reason she took each no as a direct slap against her salesmanship. She knew she wasn't being realistic, but she couldn't help herself. Canvassing was the first rule of thumb for any successful real estate office.

Her dark eyes scanned the new listings a second time. They were all small clapboard houses with no real property to speak of. Adam Noble wouldn't be interested in any of them with the exception of one possibility, and it was slim at best.

Carly glanced at the office clock. If she hurried, she could call the owner and take a quick run out to Orchard Lane and take a look at the twelve-room house that her mother had listed just a week ago. Melissa had a way of making a shack sound like the house of one's dreams. Her eyes scanned the printed form that listed the acreage of the property. It sounded good, certainly room enough for a pool and tennis court. Landscaped by a professional. Country kitchen. That should please Adam. A smile tugged at the corners of Carly's mouth. Adam. The name pleased her. The man himself intrigued her. Did she please him? Or was that interest he showed her at the restaurant merely courtesy on his part? Did she, for that matter, want his interest to be anything other than that?

"I think it's time to call it a day," her mother called from behind the real estate section of the paper she was scanning.

"It's all right with me, Mother. I think I'll take a ride out to the Barlow property you listed last week and take a look around. I think I might have a buyer for it. Actually, I should have said possible buyer. How much of this write-up is frosting, Mother? Is the place as good as it sounds?"

"Carly, for shame! It's everything I wrote down on the form. Of course, it needs some work," she added hastily at Carly's suspicious look.

"How much work, Mother? In terms of money, how much?" Carly asked tartly.

"Five, maybe seven thousand. Who can say? It depends on who is doing the buying and what they want to change," Melissa answered airily.

"Let me put it to you another way, Mother. If I was the one who was considering the purchase of this property, how much would I have to pay for improvements to make the house livable?"

"Darling, you have such plebeian tastes. You wouldn't change a thing. You adore all that rustic rusty nonsense."

"I guess that means the place is falling down," Carly snapped. "Now, why didn't you just tell me that in the beginning, and you could have saved us both aggravation."

"I'm not aggravated, darling. You're the one who is aggravated," Melissa said checking her makeup in a tiny compact. "You've been in this business enough to know you have to gild the lily a little. Go out and check it out yourself. It's a handyman's dream, and the price is . . ."

"Utterly ridiculous," Carly shot back, annoyed with her mother's airy words.

"Is it my fault that the Barlows want to retire to Paradise Island and run a charter fishing outfit? I didn't set the price, they did."

"You certainly didn't discourage them, did you?"

"Good heavens, no. After all, I would like the highest possible commission. Darling, properties like the Barlows' don't fall into your lap every day. Foresight is what's called for here on the part of the buyer."

"Foresight!" Carly exclaimed.

"Somewhere, some place, there is someone who is just waiting to see the Barlow property, and that someone will think it's the house of his dreams. I personally guarantee it."

Carly gave up and settled back in her chair. It didn't pay to argue with her mother. "Okay, I'll close up and see you later. I am going to call the Barlows and stop by on my way home. Don't wait dinner for me."

"I won't. I'm just going to pop a potpie into the microwave for myself and, darling," she called over her shoulder, "stretch that seven thousand to ten." The door closed behind her with a curt slam that set Carly's teeth on edge.

"Motheeerrr," Carly groaned aloud. The last comment told her she shouldn't even bother making the trip to the Barlows'. Still, she didn't have anything else to do so why not stop by? At least she could see with her own eyes what condition the property was in. If the Barlows had any kind of business acumen, they might be willing to make some improvements themselves to entice a buyer to meet their price. Paradise Island, no less, she sniffed to herself, deciding to cancel the whole idea. What she really wanted was to go home. Take off her shoes, relax in a hot tub. Slamming her desk drawer shut and covering her typewriter, she decided that was exactly what she would do.

A wrinkled apple in one hand and her briefcase in the other, Carly headed for her room to draw that hot bath.

Submerged in the fragrant, steamy water, she let her mind wander back to her lunch with Adam Noble. He certainly was a handsome man, a powerful man with great magnetism. And she had been completely wrong about him. He did do more than just breathe. During their lunch he had told her that until recently he had held a position as a public defender and had maintained a small law practice. Since abandoning those projects he was now busy making contacts helpful toward a political career and learning the ins and outs of campaigning.

With his background and family connections he was a natural to run for the seat in the Senate. And she would bet her last dollar that he would win. People like Adam, who had his charisma, always came out on top. She would probably vote for him herself.

He hadn't actually told her why he wanted such a large house. Was he planning on getting married? The thought was disconcerting. She wasn't certain she liked the idea of knocking herself out to look for just the right house so he could share it with some other woman.

"Bells ringing! Bells ringing!" Quincy screeched as he fluttered into the bathroom and then out.

"I hear it, I hear it," Carly yelled as she stepped from the bath and wrapped herself in a lime green terry robe. She dabbed at the perspiration on her forehead with her sleeve as she padded downstairs to the front door. Melissa must have forgotten her key as usual, or else she was too lazy to dig in her purse to find it. She caught sight of her hair piled in a topknot on her head in the foyer mirror as she opened the door. Quincy lighted on her shoulder and blended with the lime robe. "Life is hell! War is hell!" he babbled as Carly tried to shake him loose.

Carly's eyes widened. Oh, why me? Why now? Adam Noble stood framed in the doorway, Simone at his side.

There was a smile in his eyes as he stared at the girl in the doorway. "This will take but a moment. Late this afternoon a friend of mine told me the Newsome house is due to go up for sale in a few days. I thought if you went out there ahead of the other realtors we might be able to work something out. I apologize for coming by, but I thought you might want to get an early start in the morning."

Carly swallowed hard, aware of how she must look compared to Simone Maddox who looked as though she had just stepped from the pages of the latest *Vogue* magazine.

"Fine, fine," she mumbled. "I'll look into it in the morning. Tha...thank you for stopping by to tell me."

"We thought you would be interested," Simone said coyly as she tightened her grip on Adam's arm. It was clear she felt she had nothing to fear from Carly in her lime green robe and perspiring face. "Your bird is adorable. Does he fly south in the winter?"

"Only if he has a reservation at the Fontainebleu," Carly snapped. Her tart tone went unnoticed by the woman who tugged at Adam's arm.

"We'll be late, darling, and you know how the judge gets upset if I don't play at least one game of chess with him before he retires for the night." She inclined her head in Carly's direction and tugged again on Adam's arm. He seemed about to say something and Carly waited. Instead, he smiled warmly, apologized again and walked into the darkness with his companion.

Carly closed the door and seethed with anger. It was *her* idea, Carly knew it; she could feel it. She was a witch. Somehow, she knew I'd be in this tacky robe, looking like a ragamuffin, and that's why she had him stop by. So he could compare. She snorted indignantly, what comparison? "You're right, Quincy, life is hell," she snarled as she made her way back upstairs.

At least part of her question was answered. The woman was right at home with the Noble family if she played chess with the judge every night. Was she staying in the Noble mansion? Was she engaged to Adam Noble? Prospective daughters-in-law would definitely play chess with a prospective father-in-law. Though Simone looked as though she didn't have a brain in her head. She also probably cheated or deliberately let the judge win so she could ingratiate herself within the family. She was a tricky one all right. Melissa would have seen through her in a minute and put her in her place. There was no doubt about it; she had been upstaged by an expert. Well, there was upstaging and there was upstaging. The next round would be hers, she would see to it.

Carly seethed and fumed the rest of the evening and only cooled down when she heard her mother's key in the lock. Then she dived beneath the covers and turned off the light. Her dreams were fitful, filled with ravishing-looking women chasing Adam Noble along the bay. She was not one of the parade of women. She was standing on the sidelines with tears streaming down her cheeks. Her mother was behind her waving a chessboard overhead, screeching that if she had only learned to play chess she could be one of the chasing women.

Carly woke instantly. For a moment she felt disoriented and puzzled. She never woke before the alarm next to her bed shrilled. She knew something was about to happen, she didn't know how she knew, she just knew. When the phone next to her bed rang, she caught it on the first ring. "Hello," she said cautiously, stealing a peek at the clock near the phone. Five A.M.!

"Miss Andrews, this is Adam Noble. I apologize for calling at this ungodly hour, but I was wondering if you would be interested in viewing a sunrise with me. I know it's a bit early and that I woke you, and I do apologize."

Carly was stunned. View a sunrise with Adam Noble! And he apologized for waking her! Cool, she had to play it cool. "I'd like that very much, Mr. Noble."

"Would you really?" he asked in a surprised voice. "I debated calling you and then I said to myself, Carly looks like the kind of gal who likes to see a sunrise. I want to take you to a favorite spot of mine. I'll pick you up in ten minutes. Can you be ready?"

"It's no problem. I adore sunrises and sunsets. I'm always up at this time of day," Carly fibbed, "and, yes, I can be ready in ten minutes."

"Good, I'll be the guy in the red car, standing in front of your house. I'll see you in ten minutes then. And, Carly, you promised to call me Adam."

"I'll be waiting, Adam," Carly said happily into the phone.

A streak of lightning had nothing on Carly as she threw on her clothes and quickly washed and brushed her teeth. She was running a comb through her hair as she ran down the stairs. She was tapping her foot on the driveway when Adam Noble skidded to a stop. He leaned across the seat to open the door for her, and Carly slid into the bucket seat. She grinned. "I don't know why, but I feel as though I'm playing hooky or something."

Adam laughed, a full rich sound that delighted Carly. "It goes with getting up early and watching the sun come up. It's my favorite time of day. What's your favorite time of day, Carly?"

She wanted to say any time as long as you figure in the time span, but she didn't. "I think I like sunsets the best. Have you ever been to Key West?" At Adam's nod, she continued. "I'm not that well traveled, but I think that the Keys have the most gorgeous sunsets I've ever seen. There's a sort of peacefulness about viewing a sunset. It's the end of the day, that kind of thing," Carly finished lamely. She should have said she preferred sunrises.

Adam laughed again. "How did you like the Keys?"

"Fantastic," Carly exclaimed. "I took the tour through Ernest Hemingway's house. I don't think I would want to live there with the only water supply coming from that one pipe though. And that bridge! The less said about it the better."

Adam frowned. "Do you have some kind of fear about water?" Adam asked, a strange note in his voice.

"No, not really, why do you ask?"

There was a relieved note in Adam's tone. "Because I'm taking you for a ferry ride to see something special; at least, it's special to me. If we luck out and catch the first ferry, we'll make it to land just as the sun comes over the horizon."

"Where are we going?"

"To a special place as I said. It's no secret really. Everyone hereabouts knows that the Sinclaires have the most beautiful piece of property in these parts. Martha Sinclaire is my godmother and from the time I was a small boy that house was a second home to me. I even have my own set of keys," he said, pointing to the dashboard. "Hop out, we're here. Looks like we'll be the only passengers," Adam said cutting the engine.

Carly hopped out as she was told and was suddenly overcome with shyness when Adam took her hand in preparation to running toward the ferry.

How warm and strong his hand felt. A sudden overwhelming sense of freedom coursed through her as she gripped his hand to show that she was aware of him and the closeness they were sharing.

Aside from the helmsman and pilot the ferry was desolate as it prepared for its initial run of the day across the bay. It serviced the small community of Deer Island and brought commuters over to the mainland where they worked. Later in the day two more trips would be made before the final voyage at nine o'clock. There would be an hour and a half layover at the island so Carly knew it would be after seven-thirty before she arrived back in Bar Harbor.

The ride on the ferry took nearly half an hour as they chugged across a metallic gray inlet of the bay over to Deer Island whose lush green grasses and gentle hills rose about the blue Atlantic and saved for itself a gull's eye view of the bluffs of Bar Harbor. Early morning sea birds, intent on finding breakfast, swooped and played in the eddies of wind created by the churning prop. Their voices were mournful and melodious, breaking the quiet of the new day just as they broke the gray of morning and the first light glinted off their outspread wings.

Adam led Carly from the ferry landing, tugging on her arm. "Hurry. Come on. We have to run. We just have a few minutes."

Carly nodded and started off on a sprint, glad she had worn blue jeans and sneakers. She ran beside the long-legged Adam and was winded by the time they reached a small rise at the end of the Sinclaires' property. Adam was breathing evenly and grinning at the same time. "City girl," he teased, as he turned her to face the eastern sky, standing behind her, his hands placed lightly on her shoulders.

It was a long moment before he spoke, and when he did, his tone was hushed. His lips were so near to her ear that Carly started. "When I watch the sun come up, I wish I was a writer, but I still don't think I could ever describe the mysteries or the colors of dawn."

"That's because you're trying to describe your emotions, not the colors."

Adam turned her around and looked down into her face, that strange, mysterious expression making shadows in his indigo eyes. His voice was husky when he spoke. "You're right, you're absolutely right. All these years I've wanted to describe what a sunrise from this spot on Deer Island was like, and I've never found the words."

Carly heard a kind of wonder and understanding in his tone, and it sent shivers up her spine. His hand tilted her chin upwards so she could look into the indigo depths of his eyes, and she saw herself reflected there. And deeper, much deeper, beyond the shadows and light, was an emotion that seemed to steal her breath away. Gently, he enfolded her in his arms, drawing her nearer, blocking out all awareness of beauty around them. He filled her gaze and became her world. And when his lips touched hers, it was softly, so softly, and she could have wondered if she were imagining that this was happening if it were not for the strong, unyielding strength of his embrace and the stir of emotions and dizzy soaring of her heart.

As the sun crept over the horizon and shed its golden light over them, Adam's lips warmed hers, igniting in her a desire she had never known she possessed. And she basked in that light, felt it reflected in her. Higher and higher, he took her with him, like the sun on its endless journey across the sky, bursting forth in celestial splendor until the fires within her blazed beside his own.

When he released her, she was lost, abandoned, cold, feeling as though the daylight had been stolen from her. But when she looked into his eyes once again, she saw the embers of a fire banked and glowing, ready to explode once again if she would only step into his arms. Struggling for control of her emotions, she murmured, "You're missing the sunrise, Adam." His name came so easily to her lips. The lips where the burning impression of his kiss still lingered.

Adam smiled, a rich, warm smile that made Carly smile in return. Suddenly, Adam threw back his head and laughed, the laugh that delighted Carly. "I guess you know we missed the sunrise. I brought you all the way out here to see a sunrise and we missed it." He looked at his watch. "All we have time for now is a walk through the gardens, and then I have to get back to town. I wish you could see the inside of the house, but it's impossible. Perhaps, another time."

"I'd like that, Adam. If the inside is anything like the outside, I know why you love this place and it's special to you."

"You have no idea how special this place really is. My mother died when I was five years old. Martha Sinclaire was a surrogate mother to me. It seems I ferried over here every day of my life until I left for college. I think I would sell my soul to own this place; that's how much it means to me."

"Do you think they'll ever sell it?" Carly asked.

"There have been rumors that that is what they're planning. If it ever does go up for sale, I would buy it in a second."

"I'm sure that if the property ever does go on the market, you're the first person the Sinclaires will think of," Carly said in a consoling tone.

"Not likely, Carly. Malcolm Sinclaire and my father had a disagreement a few years back and haven't spoken a word since. I tried to be fair about the matter but found myself siding with my father. Malcolm has a tendency to be stiff-necked. He knows how fond I am of Martha, his wife. Him too, for that matter. If this house ever does go on the market, Malcolm will do it through an agency. That's the way he does things. At that point I would have to be there, johnny-on-the-spot, that kind of thing. Fortunately, he hasn't allowed his pride to prompt him to forbid my seeing Martha but I'm afraid even that has become an uncomfortable situation for both of us. Martha is unbendingly loyal to her husband. Someday, I hope the situation will be rectified; until then, I'll just have to wait."

Carly giggled. "Adam Noble, you have nothing to worry about. My mother plays bridge with Martha Sinclaire, and if there's one thing you can say about my mother, she's johnny-on-the-spot when it comes to listing properties. I think it's safe to promise you first crack at the deal if it ever happens."

Adam sighed as he led Carly around the rock garden. "Anything else would always be second best. This is what I want—where I belong. I can't explain it any other way."

"You don't have to. I understand. You feel it's part of you, part of your childhood, your youth. Part of your life. You've come full circle now, and you want to put down your roots. It's understandable that you would come to the place that has made you the happiest."

Adam stopped in mid-stride and turned to face Carly. His face wore the same expression it had back on the atoll. "What you said, just now, it's true. I have come full circle."

Carly felt herself begin to tremble. Was he going to kiss her again? She swallowed hard as Adam's eyes bored into hers. "Did...did I say...say something wrong?" she asked in a tight little voice.

"On the contrary. You said something very right. Come, we have to get back. We'll come here again, I promise you that."

Chapter Four

Carly spent the balance of the day in a near daze. She couldn't believe the moments she had spent with Adam on Deer Island. The kiss, the closeness, the wanting to learn more about him.

From time to time Melissa looked at her and shook her head. It was simply amazing how much busywork Carly could find when something was either troubling her or was going so well that she was afraid that her own personal "jinx" would rise and spoil it all.

Melissa's close scrutiny did not go unnoticed by Carly. Right now, this very second, her mother was dying to know more about her early morning trip with Adam Noble. How could she talk about it so soon when it was something she wanted to keep to herself and cherish? To hold it close like in her childhood days when she found a treasure she wanted to savor alone. Now wasn't the time to confide in Melissa.

Carly knew she was doing busywork by filling out forms, straightening out files, watering plants and emptying trash. Repeat phone calls to follow up work could also be classified as busywork. All of it contrived to keep her moving, to keep her from thinking. What she really wanted to do was to lean back in her chair and recapture the moments with Adam.

Melissa frowned, uncertain if she should speak to Carly. As the dreamy expression on her daughter's face brought a smile to her lips, she went back to her own tedious job of sorting through three months of bank statements.

The phone, when it rang, seemed to be muted and come from far away. Without wasted motion, she reached out for the receiver. "Andrews Realty."

"Carly, Adam. I realize this is short notice but I was wondering if you would like to take a ride out to the Fisherman for Maine lobster and sourdough biscuits."

Carly's arm tingled as she held the receiver to her ear. Just the sound of his voice did strange things to her. Her voice was nearly breathless when she replied. "I'd like that very much, Adam." Out of the corner of her eye she watched a smile play across Melissa's face. Good mother that she was, it was evident that for once she wasn't going to ask any questions.

"Good, I was hoping you'd say 'yes.' If it's all right with you, I'll pick you up at the office. All I ask is that you bring a hearty appetite with you. I understand that the smallest lobster is something close to three pounds. And as you know, the biscuits are made on the hour and they're hot and dripping with butter."

Carly laughed. How deep his voice was, how sure and confident. Again, she felt the breathlessness coming over her. This was exactly the way she had felt when she was in the eighth grade and had a crush on the football hero of the junior high. Swallowing hard, she forced herself to relax. "I think I can promise that I'll have a very hearty appetite. You're talking about two of my favorite foods."

"Six o'clock then?"

There was a catch in her voice when she answered. "Fine."

"Carly?"

"Yes?"

"I'm not a very wordy person as you must have noticed this morning. I want you to know that I enjoyed missing the sunrise with you."

"Hmm," was all Carly could dare with Melissa hanging on every word. "Six o'clock then. I'll be ready and so will my appetite. That's a warning."

Adam chuckled. "That's all I ask. See you later."

Carly replaced the phone. It wasn't until moments later that she realized she hadn't said goodbye. A nervous giggle erupted in her throat. She felt light-headed with the knowledge that in just a short time she would be sitting next to Adam. They would dine together and after that, as in true romantic fiction they would walk along the rocky strip of beach. It was almost one of the requirements of the Fisherman. Leisurely cocktails, gourmet salad bar and then the serious business of devouring the specialty of the house; Maine lobster and sourdough biscuits. The patrons were left with no other choice but to walk off the calories. It was standard fare for the patrons of the Fisherman and one or two of Carly's old friends had admitted that the intimate strolls along the beach had direct bearing on their engagements to the men of their choice.

"Going out, darling?" Melissa asked casually as she folded the hateful bank statements that refused to balance according to her records.

Carly couldn't help herself. A wide grin split her face. "Adam Noble invited me to dinner. He's picking me up at six."

"That's nice, Carly, have a nice time. Make certain he follows the tradition of the Fisherman and takes you for a walk along the beach."

"Mother, who said anything about going to the Fisherman?"

"You didn't have to. It's the nicest restaurant in town and where else would Adam Noble take you? I hear the smallest lobster is three pounds. Darling, whatever you do, don't eat the whole thing. It's so tacky to see women digging into a lobster the way men do. Try to be dainty. I'm not saying you're sloppy, Carly, it's just that you have to wear the bibs and the drawn butter does dribble. Your fingers get all messy and you constantly have to use those little wet cloths. Not ladylike at all." Melissa pursed her lips to show her disapproval. Even though she dearly loved fresh lobster she would never subject herself to wearing a bib in public or wiping her hands on what she called little wet pieces of paper.

"Oh, I will mother. Don't worry about me. I intend to dive into that lobster and I'll eat each and every morsel savoring it to the fullest. If I should look tacky I won't let it bother me. After all, the main purpose of going to the Fisherman is to indulge. I'm certain that Adam will be too busy savoring his to notice me. I know how to behave in public," Carly assured Melissa, "you did bring me up with all the proper manners."

Melissa preened at the compliment. She really had done a good job with Carly. Actually, the job must have worked out better than she had even suspected if Adam Noble was interested in her little girl. He had a reputation for dating only the most glamorous society girls. She sniffed. Carly could hold her own anywhere once she made up her mind to it. "Darling, just enjoy the evening. If you want to gorge, then do so, by all means."

"I intend to," Carly answered brightly. "Go along now and take care of Quincy. I can finish up here. I'll even go over those bank statements for you. Adam is picking me up here at the office so I might as well keep busy until he gets here."

"Carly, you are a darling child. I thought you'd never ask. I left the statements in the drawer for you. I never saw such a hodgepodge of numbers. Sometimes banks are so unreasonable. Now, you enjoy yourself and don't be late. Tomorrow is a working day." With an airy wave of her slender hand, Melissa was gone, her perfume lingering in the office.

Carly sighed. It was nice to be alone. She had an hour to kill before Adam picked her up. First, she would freshen up and apply some casual makeup for evening wear and then she would get down to the bank statements. In a way, it would be a welcome relief to really concentrate on something important. This way, she couldn't keep thinking about Adam and the morning sunrise.

Deftly, Carly applied fresh blusher to her high cheekbones. A slight smidgin of charcoal liner and just a dab of eye shadow. She stood back to see the effect. Just a trace more mascara and some lip gloss. Thank heavens she had dressed with extra care this morning after she had returned from Deer Island. Almost as if she had had a premonition of this evening. More like wishful thinking, she told herself.

The mulberry sheath with contrasting orchid belt set off her slim figure to perfection. A golden expanse of leg flashed as the linenlike fabric parted at the knee. It was dressy, yet casual. She felt satisfied as she straightened the slim gold chain at her neck, her only concession to jewelry aside from the gold circlet on her wrist.

The only thing missing now was a dab of perfume behind each ear and again at the base of her throat. She searched through her purse and found the tiny vial of Balmain perfume she always carried with her for an occasion like this.

The door opened suddenly while Carly was frowning at her mother's penciled numbers. A look of exasperation crossed her pretty face. She was so engrossed in trying to decipher the figures Adam Noble had to speak twice before she heard him.

Quickly, she gathered up the statements into a neat pile and then shoved them into the drawer. The deep indigo eyes were making her feel strange again, washing her over with an almost uncontrollable desire to fling herself into his arms. "I really am sorry. I was so engrossed in what I was doing I didn't hear you come in." Thank goodness simple words could take the edge off her emotions.

He smiled to show he understood. Suddenly, she felt comfortable with him again, just like during the early morning hours they had spent together. The breathless tight feeling in her chest was gone.

One smile from him and she felt like a new woman. The only woman, in Adam Noble's eyes.

The short ride to the Fisherman was made with small talk. Adam had a keen wit and Carly laughed as he expounded on some of his childhood exploits with his brother Cayce.

The interior of the Fisherman was dim. Wide lengths of fishnets hung from the open beams with starfish attached to the netting. Japanese floats sparkled, reflecting the light from the lanterns.

A stunning hostess in a trim sailor suit greeted Adam with a warm smile that embraced Carly at the same time. "Please follow me and watch your step. It's rather dim in here until you get used to the lighting."

Carly followed the hostess's sure-footed stride with Adam following. A hanging fishnet that made each booth private was parted for Carly to enter. As always, when coming to the Fisherman she marveled at the beauty of the pewter serviceware and the subtle gleam of the silver. The tiny hurricane lamp with its miniature candle danced in the slight breeze the fishnet made when closing. How intimate this setting was. How nice of Adam to suggest it.

Settling back into the softness of the leather booth Carly let her gaze lock with Adam's for a moment. It was impossible to feel so drawn to a man so quickly, she told herself, yet that was exactly what was happening. A strange, new emotion was kindled within her, a yearning, a kind of hunger, a hunger that all the Maine lobster in the world would never satisfy. A warm flush stained her cheeks as Adam gazed into her eyes. Just then, the waitress arrived for their cocktail order.

"A Banana Daiquiri," she said to Adam.

"I'll have Scotch on the rocks and a Banana Daiquiri for the lady."

How husky his voice was, how sensual. Damn, here she was letting her emotions and her attraction for the man run away with her again. She should come down to earth instead of sitting opposite him smiling into space.

"You're beautiful in the candlelight, Carly. I've been remiss in complimenting you. You look lovely this evening."

Carly blushed prettily. Compliments always threw her off her stride. But she remembered Melissa's advice. Turn the compliment around, accept it graciously. "Thank you, Adam. How nice of you to say so."

His voice had been sincere, warm and flattering. Interested. Was it possible that he was as attracted to her as she was toward him?

The drinks arrived. Noiselessly, the fishnet separated. Conversation was suspended as the glasses were placed in front of them. The waitress stepped back waiting for them to sample the drinks. Adam nodded his approval and looked at Carly who nodded. "Delicious," she said. Discreetly, the waitress withdrew, leaving them alone once again. Conversation was easy as they commented on the season, the various restaurants and the gaggle of tourists that invaded their habitat of Bar Harbor each year.

"I hate to move but I guess if we want to eat we're going to have to go into the dining room and choose our lobsters and tackle the salad bar. There's no hurry, but I warn you, I'm a starving man. Take pity on me, Carly. Finish your drink and follow me."

Once more the lacy netting parted and Adam stepped aside for Carly to make her way to the lobster trough. With great deliberation, Adam scrutinized each and every lobster that moved crankily in the swirling water. He finally selected one, saying it was an exemplary specimen and waited for Carly to make her choice. Satisfied that she had picked one to equal his own, he cupped her elbow in his hand and led her to the elaborately arranged salad bar.

Carly bypassed the standard garden vegetables and concentrated on the clams on the half shell, deviled crab and plump, pink shrimp. Adam followed suit adding only real bacon bits to his small helping of garden salad. Conversation was animated as they devoured the tender seafood. "Carly," Adam said suddenly, "is it possible for you to take the afternoon off tomorrow?" Not waiting for a reply, he rushed on. "I'd like you to come out to the house for lunch and some fun. My brothers are all in town, which is a rarity in itself. We so rarely find ourselves under the same roof that when we do, it's cause for celebration. The judge, now that he's older, lives for these little get-togethers. What do you say, think you can arrange it?"

Carly was stunned. He was actually inviting her to his home to meet his family. Melissa always said that when a man took a girl home it meant he was interested in pursuing the relationship. "I don't see why not. I more or less got caught up with my work yesterday. I'd like to meet your family, Adam."

"That's good. It's settled then. I'll pick you up a little after noon. Wear old clothes and we'll make a day of it. Lunch is always very informal. As a matter of fact, you really need a long arm to leave the table with any food under your belt when everyone is home. Shyness is equated with starvation, around the Noble home. My brothers live to eat. Just like me," he smiled. "It might be a little tough for you to adjust to their exuberance but they all mean well. And children, I hope you're crazy about children because there's a herd of them around our place just now and we all think they're important enough to deserve all the attention they demand...." His voice was soft, even a little shy as he gazed at her. "I just wanted to warn you about what you're getting yourself into if you join the Noble clan for the afternoon. I guess I've done a good job of scaring you away."

Excitement gripped Carly. "I'm an only child. I remember growing up wishing I had a dozen brothers and sisters. I know I'll enjoy meeting your 'clan' as you call them. And thank you for inviting me. I'm looking forward to it. Casual clothes, right?"

"Right. Jeans and sneakers. A windbreaker in case the afternoon cools off. I hear a storm is brewing south of us. Trust me, I know at times I seem overpowering to you. Being the youngest of all my brothers I had to yell the loudest, fight the hardest and be the best to get any kind of notice at all. I guess I haven't really outgrown all those childhood traits. Not faults, just traits,'' he teased.

In that one moment Carly felt closer to him than she had in the time she had known him. How dear he was. How wonderful he made her feel just being with him and listening to him talk. He could recite nursery rhymes and she knew she would still think he was the most interesting man she had ever met. Her mind and heart soared with a new elation that was washing over her. A tiny niggle of apprehension tried to warn her; too quick, too fast. Slow down, Carly. Adam Noble was the big leagues. She was Carly Andrews, little league.

''It's nice to meet someone who isn't perfect. Wait, let me revise that. Nice to meet someone who admits to being imperfect,'' she teased.

''And you, Carly. What about you? What do you want out of life?''

''Oh, I don't know. I think I've been in some kind of holding pattern or at least, that's what my mother tells me. For now I'm doing a job that I like and doing it to the best of my ability. I like to think I take care of my mother and then there's Quincy who somehow or another got to be my sole responsibility. He does keep me hopping and at the same time he's great company. I guess that more or less sums up Carly Andrews and just in time. Here come our lobsters.'' Was she imagining it or did Adam seem disappointed? Whatever the expression was in his eyes, it was too short-lived to put a name to it.

''I've been waiting for this all day,'' Adam said gleefully as he allowed the waitress to attach an oversized paper bib with a large red lobster printed on the front around his neck. ''Don't say it,'' he laughed as the waitress turned to Carly and shook out the folded bib. ''Don't say how cute I look.''

''I won't,'' Carly promised, ''not unless you tell me first.''

The waitress laughed saying, ''Enjoy your dinner. If you want anything else, just press the buzzer at the side of the table.''

Adam nodded as he turned the lobster around on his plate trying to decide if he should attack the claws or the tail first. His eyes danced with laughter as he watched Carly do the same thing. ''You look like a little cherub sitting there.''

Carly couldn't help it, she burst out laughing. ''I was thinking you look like an overgrown baby waiting for his mother to tell him it's okay to dig in.'' They looked at each other, happy, contented, excited.

It was one of the most enjoyable evenings Carly had ever spent. While Adam paid the check she skipped off to the powder room to repair her makeup. Not wanting to delay the walk on the beach that she was certain was forthcoming, she made her way to the front of the restaurant that was jam-packed with diners who hadn't had the foresight to make a reservation. Adam's eyes seemed to light at the sight of her.

"What do you say to a walk along the beach?"

"I'll have to take my shoes off," Carly told him, looking down at her spike heeled shoes.

"So will I," he confided. "We'll walk along the mud flats. Away from the rocks. You can't eat at the Fisherman and not take your girl down to the beach. And you can't abandon a tradition as old as time itself."

"Fine, I get the message," Carly giggled as she slipped out of her thin heeled slippers. Gallantly, Adam reached for them and stuck one in each of his pockets. "Does that make you feel like Cinderella?"

"Of course. But I promise I don't turn into a pumpkin at midnight. At the stroke of twelve I'm still Carly Andrews."

They held hands as they walked along the hard mud flats, the wet, dark brown sand seeping between their toes. Carly loved every minute of it. Adam seemed to be enjoying himself too. She had half expected that he would take her in his arms and kiss her. But he didn't, but Carly didn't mind. It was so nice just walking beside him, knowing he was content with her company. And there was still tomorrow to look forward to. He must like her a little at least, otherwise he wouldn't be taking her to meet his family.

"I think it's time to head back. The lighthouse is just ahead and we've come pretty far. I don't want to tire you out. You have a big day tomorrow."

"It is getting late," Carly agreed as she turned to start back in the direction from which they'd come. Adam slowed a moment and caught her in his arms. A sound erupted in Carly's throat and smothered as Adam's lips found hers. It was a light feathery kiss demanding nothing but accepting all she cared to give. She was shaken to her toes when he released her. They gazed at one another through the darkness and then walked on. Words weren't necessary. They continued their lazy, contented walk back to the concrete area where a small foot bath had been installed. Carly sat down on the slatted bench while Adam poured water over her feet and then toweled them with the coarse paper towels. Other couples were strolling the beach, lost in one another, walking hand in hand, just as she had done with Adam.

"And that's the end to one of the nicest evenings I've spent in a long time," Adam said as he led her to the parking lot. "You really have to commend me, I'll have you home on the stroke of midnight."

"How cavalier of you, sir," Carly quipped as she slid into the low-slung bucket seat.

The ride home was much too short for Carly. Adam walked her to the door and held out his hand for her key. He fitted it into the lock and swung the door open. He squeezed her hand gently for a moment and then turned to sprint down the flagstone walk. Carly could hear him whistling before he turned on the engine. She smiled into the darkness as she made her way up the staircase to her room. "And a good time was had by all," she said softly. "Especially by me."

Carly awoke, completely aware of her surroundings. No morning grogginess for her. She knew exactly what day it was and what was on the agenda for her in the afternoon. Excitement raced through her veins as she headed for the shower. She lathered up briskly and washed her silky hair. After all, she did want to look her best even if she was going to wear jeans and sneakers.

Coffee was perking merrily and Quincy was sputtering as he flew about the kitchen in search of his breakfast. "Feed me, Carly. Carly is a good girl," he cackled as he buzzed the top of her head before lighting on top of the refrigerator. He swooped down on Melissa who banged her shin as she tried to evade him.

"Darling, just one morning can't we keep that bird in his cage until I've had my morning coffee? Just one morning of peace and quiet."

"Don't you want to hear about my evening, mother?"

"By the expression on your face I don't have to ask," Melissa quipped. "You look like you not only had a pleasant evening but are aware that there are more evenings to come."

"I'm taking the afternoon off, mother. Adam invited me to lunch since his brothers and sisters are in town. I knew you wouldn't mind. I really am caught up with the office work. I even took a stab at straightening out the bank statements. If you bring them home I'll do them before I go to bed."

"What more could a mother ask," Melissa retorted as she brought the coffee cup to her lips. "It never ceases to amaze me that a little caffeine can make the world right side up. Why aren't you drinking your coffee, Carly?"

"I will, mother. Do you think it's strange that Adam invited me to meet his family?"

"Not at all, darling. Men do that when they're interested in a girl. At least they did in my day and I'm not all that old. I don't think times have changed all that much. I think it's grand."

"Don't you think I'll be out of place if Simone is there? After all, I'm not quite sure what the relationship is between her and Adam."

"Darling, that is not your problem. It's Adam's. I'm sure he wouldn't have invited you if something...something was going on between them. Take it from your mother, Carly. You have nothing to worry about. If anything, I would say that Simone should do the worrying."

Carly impulsively threw her arms around her mother. "Thanks, Mom, I really needed to hear that."

"Carly, never sell yourself short. Darling, you're real, not like some of those high-powered ambitious fashion-model types that parade around the Harbor during the summer. They fade like autumn leaves. What I'm saying, dear, is blood runs through your veins, not chlorophyll. Understand?"

"I know, Mother, but remember, you're prejudiced. Look, I'm not going to jump into anything. So far, this is nothing more than a pleasant time for me. I enjoy Adam's company. He seems to enjoy mine. If there's going to be more it will come, slow and natural. If it doesn't work out then I'll have had a few pleasant memories to store away for a rainy day."

"That's the perfect attitude to adopt, Carly," Melissa agreed with maternal pride. "I really did do a super job of raising you. Sometimes I'm so proud of you, like now, that I want to go outside and shout it to the world what a great girl I raised."

"They already know. Old Mr. Snyder tells me that all the time when he sees me mow the lawn. He said there aren't too many people who can cut the grass with a parrot perched on the grass catcher. Thanks for the compliment."

Carly watched the clock all morning. At eleven-thirty she retired to the powder room to change into jeans and sneakers. A lemon yellow sweatshirt was her only concession to color.

Melissa stared at her and sighed. "For a minute there you looked like a fifteen-year-old heading for cheerleading practice. I think I just got misty-eyed. I just saw a flash of red pull up on the street. Enjoy yourself, Carly."

"I will, Mother. Hold down the fort. I'll see you sometime tonight. Can't promise when."

Melissa waved airily as Carly skipped out to the car.

"Don't tell me, you're a canary, right?" Adam teased, pointing to her yellow shirt.

"Thank you," Carly settled in beside him, offering Adam a wry smile.

Not too much later, Carly found herself being introduced to Adam's brothers. Each shook her proffered hand and grinned the fabulous Noble grin as they welcomed her to the "clan." She felt welcomed and accepted by all of them. Their manner was easy and comfortable, like Adam's. The Noble women were busy with their children who played on the wide expanse of green lawn out back but they each came over to meet her and say hello.

It was Cayce who bid for her to be on his team for a rousing game of touch football. The judge and a solemn-faced Simone sat on the sidelines with glasses of carrot juice in their hands.

"Feint, Carly, that's it. Good girl! Swivel now! You've got it!" Brock yelled as Adam tackled her.

Laughing, Carly fell to the ground only to reach out, grab the ball and run like lightning.

"This way, Carly! Wrong way, Carly! That's it, you've got it. Run! Run! Wow! Adam, did you see her run? Great stuff," Cayce called to her as she tumbled over the line that made the touchdown legitimate.

"Hey!" Carly complained playfully. "I thought this was touch ball. No tackling!"

"Not the way we Nobles play. We've got our own rules!"

"Believe him, Carly," Adam's sister Helen advised. "All the Nobles play by their own rules."

"You can play on my team anytime," Brock and Cayce said as they each put an arm around her. "Wherever you found her, Adam, don't lose her. We haven't won against your side since we've come home. Come on, you guys, get the lead out. We've got three more quarters to go."

Carly giggled as she assumed the three point stance. Her eyes were bright as she glared at Adam. He was the enemy. Adam glared back. Steve, Adam and Michael took off after Carly on a dead run. Janice and Lorraine closed off the ends. Carly pivoted and then swiveled, sailing the ball high in the air to Cayce who literally leaped into the air. He was off, down the lawn for a second touchdown.

"Where did you learn to do that?" Adam demanded good naturedly.

"Just dumb luck," she retorted.

"Adam, telephone!" the housekeeper called from the patio. "Do you want to take it in the house or shall I bring the phone out here?"

"Time!" Adam called loudly.

"Poor excuse, poor loser! Some people will do anything rather than lose a game," his brothers joked as Adam sprinted back into the palatial house. Moments later, he was back, a grim expression on his face.

"What's wrong?" the judge asked, his voice gruff with concern.

"That was Martha Sinclaire. She's down in Portland getting her check-up at the medical clinic and she heard the storm warning. She wants me to go out to Deer Island and secure the skiff. You know, the one she promised to give her grandson when he graduated next year. She was having some work done on it and it's tied up at the pier. Small craft warnings are up but I couldn't refuse. You know how I feel about Martha." The judge nodded.

"Sorry fellas, this isn't intentional. I'll take the launch and be back as soon as possible. Any volunteers?" he asked as he looked pointedly at Carly.

"I can't go, Adam, I'm not dressed for it and I do so hate to get salt spray in my hair. I really don't think it's safe to be out on the water during a storm."

"Simone," Adam said in a cold voice. "I didn't ask you to go."

"I'll go with you, Adam," Carly said softly. "I was born and raised around here and know these waters almost as well as you do. You'll need someone to handle the lines to bring the skiff around. I've done it before. If you want, I'll be glad to go." She looked around for a moment and thought it strange that none of his brothers had offered to help Adam. Then she saw the grins on their faces. If they thought it was dangerous they would have insisted on going. As it was, their acceptance of her on the playing field had now carried over into something else. They wouldn't interfere. Adam also seemed to agree, even seemed pleased at her suggestion, as though he had expected it.

"Let's go then. If Martha calls back, tell her I'm on my way. Okay, Dad?"

"Right, son. Just be careful now. These storms from the south can really sweep up. And fast."

"I didn't realize we were expecting a storm," Carly said. "Guess I was too busy trying to figure out which way to run with the ball."

Adam ran along beside her as he led her to the Noble dock where he kept the launch in a tumble-down boathouse. "You did okay in that game of touch. Shame you weren't on my side. I hate to husk corn and shuck clams. That's the losing team's job."

Carly laughed as she braced herself for the first surge of power on the launch. It whipped away from the wharf leaving a froth of water behind as they headed out for open water.

Looking off to the south the sky was already dark and gloomy. The wind was rising and whipped the water into white caps. Carly had every confidence in Adam's ability as a sailor and settled down low in her seat to get as much protection from the wind as possible. The bow of the boat took on the rising swells with steadiness. Deer Island seemed worlds away as the weather continued to close in on them.

Eight minutes from landfall the storm hit full force, driving water into the open cockpit. It took all of Adam's expertise to steer the sleek craft toward land. "A few more minutes, Carly. We'll be there. I didn't expect the front to hit so soon. I don't think we'll have any trouble though. Hang on, we'll make it!" His voice carried over the whistling wind.

Carly hung on for dear life, the life vest snug around her, a comforting weight. Wind and rain slashed against her as the boat sliced through the frothing swells.

"Deer Island dead ahead. Hunker down, Carly, stay down. God, I'm sorry I brought you along. Hang on, we'll follow land to the Sinclaire dock." Carly managed a glance at Adam's face and saw the tight, grim concentration there. It was a face that instilled confidence.

"There's the boat house," he called just when Carly thought she couldn't stand another minute of the downpour. "Don't let go Carly, till I cut the engine."

She shivered as the sound of the engine died to silence. Her knuckles were sore and knotted from the grip she held on the rail. Quickly, she turned in preparation for disembarking. "Wait for me, I'll take the lines."

Fleet of foot, she jumped onto the dock and handled the lines as he worked the boat along the dock into the boat house. With the agility of a cat, he bounded to the bow and attached the hanging hook to the bowring. The stern lines attached, Adam jumped onto the walkway beside Carly and flicked the lever for the electric winch.

"Now for the skiff," Adam panted. "Think you can do it?"

Carly nodded, keeping silent. She was freezing, it was all she could do to keep her teeth from chattering.

"Good girl. Now watch the ropes, they're slippery and don't get your hands burned."

Rivers of rain washed down on them as they ran for the mooring holding the skiff. It was a light sailboat, only about twenty feet long and not too difficult to handle. Together, they walked the skiff around and directed it into the boathouse beside the launch. With quick, capable movements, Adam had it hanging from the rafters of the boathouse.

Carly was cold and weakening. She was so cold and tired she couldn't think. She just had to hold on, she told herself. And hold on she would. If only she could get out of the rain and put on some dry clothes. Adam said something about an overhead loft where they could dry off.

Every bone in her body trembling, Carly managed the rough wooden ladder that led to the loft above. She was stunned by what she saw when Adam lit the hurricane lamp on the mantel. It was a cozy one-room apartment complete with bath and wood-burning fireplace. Carly sank to the floor, every muscle in her body crying for relief.

"The bathroom's over there. You go first. There are some old beach coverups in the linen closet. While you're showering I'll build a fire and make us some coffee laced with brandy. Hurry up now before you collapse," Adam ordered in a firm voice.

Carly went off obediently. A hot shower, a fire, coffee with brandy. She was living under the right star after all.

The storm raged on as she stood under the bracing water. It continued while Adam showered and she watched the coffeepot bubble merrily. There was no sign of a let-up as they snuggled down before the dancing flames with the hot coffee mugs in their hands.

"This is unbelievable," Carly sighed. "I've heard of boat houses like this but I've never been in one."

"Martha uses it for a guesthouse sometimes. It's got all the modern conveniences, thank the Lord. By the way, don't worry about your mother worrying about you. While you were in the shower I radio-telephoned back to the mainland and Cayce will see to it that your mother is notified that you're safe and sound."

"You think of everything," Carly murmured. "You're really a very thoughtful man."

"And you're really a very pretty lady. Especially all scrubbed and cozy. I see you found something appropriate in the linen closet," he gestured toward the pale blue terry robe that had been her only choice besides skimpy bathing suits and lightweight short beach coverups.

Adam had found a pair of cutoff jeans and a ragtag tee shirt. Together they toasted their bare feet by the fire, each enjoying the warmth and companionship that going through an adventure forms between people.

"I suppose I should get up and see what's in the pantry. Getting hungry, Carly?"

"Umm. In a little bit. What's it doing outside? I can still hear the rain beating on the roof."

"Pretty nasty right about now, I suppose. Come on, let's have a look." He hefted her to her feet and together they went to the window and pulled back the gingham curtain.

The late afternoon light was gray, almost wintry, and the roiling seas were pounding the shore.

"No telling how long it will last," Carly said thoughtfully.

"No telling," Adam said, his mouth surprisingly close to her ear. Like the force of nature outside that was the wild force with which he took her in his arms. His lips came crashing down on hers, holding them, tasting them, making them a part of his own. He held her close, so closely she felt she would never again draw a breath.

He put her away from him and looked deeply into her eyes. "You're very special, Carly. Too special for a casual affair. You're the kind of girl a man marries. And that makes you extra special. To me." His voice was husky with emotion, his indigo eyes serious, plunging the depths of hers. But his smile was tender and seemed to hold a secret meaning. "I like the way you respond to me, Carly Andrews, there's no doubting that you're my kind of woman."

Carly's cheeks tingled with the heat of a flush. "You said something about a food pantry...."

"Yes, in the kitchen area. Want to see what we can find? Then I challenge you to a marathon game of Monopoly." He took her back in his arms. "And then we can have some hot chocolate and sit by the fire and fall asleep in each other's arms."

As his lips touched hers, Carly thought that she had never heard another idea that she so eagerly agreed with.

Chapter Five

Carly woke early. Dawn was now her favorite time of day since she had gone out to Deer Island with Adam, and she enjoyed it alone on the small balcony outside her bedroom window. The tiny alarm next to her bed read 6:10. The rosy hued skyline blended with the rising fog that curled and spiraled upward on the fresh sea breeze. The diamond-shaped dew drops on the close-clipped grass beneath her window shimmered and sparkled and would have been the envy of any Cartier or Tiffany jeweler.

It was a quiet time of day—a time to assess one's thinking, a time to make decisions when minds were clear and uncluttered. Not that she had decisions to make. Her life was so staid and orderly it made her sometimes feel stifled. Nothing ever happened, it seemed to Carly Andrews. She worked all day, ate dinner, washed her hair, watched television and then went to bed. The following day she would wake and do the same thing all over again. A neat, orderly, uncluttered life. Most of her friends had run off to New York to seek their fortunes. The others had married and moved away from Bar Harbor.

Carly drew a breath deep into her lungs and started her yoga exercises. She stayed with the exercises for a full thirty minutes and then showered. She felt good, felt a sense of excitement, and her adrenaline was flowing again. Amazing what an attractive man on the scene could do for a girl. A pity he was taken. Still, he wasn't married yet. If a girl had a mind to, she could fight for him. Melissa had drummed it into her head for years that anything worthwhile was worth fighting for. Could she compete with the luscious Simone and did she want to? What was there about the man, the sometime chef and possible senator that appealed to her? Obviously, he was handsome and sexy as sin itself. Some package, she mused, as she deftly applied makeup.

Carly stood back from the mirror to view her handiwork objectively. Perfect. It didn't look as though she had makeup on at all.

Adam Noble. It did have a certain ring to it. Adam Noble, attorney at law. Adam Noble, chef. Senator Adam Noble. Mrs. Adam Noble. Carly Noble! Whew! She had to stop this sort of thing. Adam Noble was spoken for. This was purely a business deal. The lunch, delightful as it had been, meant nothing to him. The fact that he stopped by meant nothing. And when he saw her in her green robe with a parrot on her shoulder. The less said the better. Carly winced remembering the picture she must have made as she opened the door. On the other hand, how often had Adam Noble knocked on a girl's door only to have it opened by a girl in a lime green robe with a parrot who shouted, "Life is hell! War is hell!"? Not too often. Suddenly, she giggled. "What you see, Mr. Noble, is what you get." She giggled again as she wondered what his elegant companion would do if Quincy ever lighted on her shoulders. Scream and faint dead away no doubt. She chided herself as she made her way to Melissa's messy kitchen.

Still, there was that hasty jaunt out to Deer Island to see the sunrise. Carly's cheeks flushed brighter. He had kissed her. She touched her fingers to her lips. No, she was being silly. It just wasn't possible that she could still feel the warmth of his mouth on hers. Besides, Adam Noble must have kissed hundreds of girls. Deer Island couldn't mean anything to him. Could it? But what about all the other kisses? her heart drummed the question. The moment in his arms when the earth stood still and Adam had become the world.

Carly looked around the untidy kitchen and made up her mind to do something about getting a housekeeper of sorts. How in the world could Melissa make such a mess heating one little potpie in a microwave oven? Carly wrapped a butcher's apron over her white linen suit and started to straighten the kitchen while her coffee perked. Orange rinds and ends of green vegetables were whisked into the garbage disposal. Odds and ends of dishes that held remnants of food that did not resemble a potpie went into the dishwasher. An electric broom whisked up all the crumbs and some of Quincy's crackers. A dishcloth that looked as though it belonged in some other war cleaned off the butcher block table. Now, she could eat her banana and have her coffee. But first she had to wake up Quincy and feed him.

"Hi. What's new?" the green bird cackled.

"Not much," Carly replied as she sipped at her instant coffee.

"Good girl," Quincy squawked as he flew wildly about the kitchen, finally lighting on top of the range hood.

"Give me one good reason why I should feed you. What do you ever do but make a mess? That's all you and Mom do, make messes that I have to clean up. Why can't you say, 'Carly's a pretty girl,' or better yet, 'Carly is a beautiful girl?' It's already been established that I'm a good girl so can we get on to bigger and better things?"

Quincy circled the kitchen and finally perched himself on Carly's arm. He looked at her with round beady eyes. "Life is hell!" he said clearly and distinctly.

"You got it, bird, it really is. But you know something? I think it's all going to change soon. Adam Noble is going to change it."

Carly looked around the kitchen. She set the coffeepot to low so her mother would have hot coffee when she awoke. Next, she checked her handbag for her car keys and her wallet to be sure she had enough cash on her for the day. Gathering up her briefcase, Carly was startled to see a bleary eyed Melissa standing in the doorway.

"Coffee..." Melissa croaked hoarsely, groping for the nearest chair while Carly hurried for cup and coffeepot.

"Mother, you look awful...."

"Yes, don't I?" Melissa smiled. "It was a glorious party and I imagine I look much the same as you did after you spent the night in the storm with Adam Noble."

Carly blushed. "I've told you, Mother. Nothing happened...."

"I can see."

"What's that supposed to mean...? Oh never mind. I don't want to hear it."

Melissa gulped her coffee. "I have some really interesting news," she said after a moment. "Martha Sinclaire told me they've decided to sell their house and move to a warmer climate. The winters are becoming too much for the poor soul.... Anyway, she stayed overnight at the Wilson's but Malcolm went home."

Carly's actions froze. The blood seemed to tingle through her veins. The Sinclaire property. On Deer Island. Adam's dream house! "Have they listed with anyone?"

"Not yet. I was hoping you'd go out there and sign it up." Slowly, Melissa was being restored to her usual bright-eyed self. "You don't have any appointments this morning, do you darling?"

Carly held her breath. She'd cancel an appointment with the Queen of England to go out to Deer Island this morning. Quickly, she picked up the phone and called downtown to the marina, making arrangements with Will Rumley to take her out in the launch.

"I'll just stop by the office and pick up a listing agreement. Will Rumley says he'll take me out there around nine-thirty." Impulsively, she kissed Melissa on the cheek and dashed for the door, her feet barely touching the ground.

Carly was working on the agreement for the Sinclaire property when Simone Maddox opened the door clad in the briefest of shorts that displayed spectacular legs.

"Hello, I was just walking by and saw you come in. Would you have an emery board? I've chipped a nail." Simone held out a scarlet tipped hand.

"I think I've got one here in my desk...." Carly murmured, opening the lower left drawer and rummaging for the emery board.

"What's this?" Simone asked curiously, picking up the listing agreement and seeing the name and Deer Island.

"Isn't this the house that Adam always raves about?"

"Yes, it is," Carly confessed. "I'm going out there to see if I can get Mr. Sinclaire to list it with me."

"You don't mind if I come along, do you? I knew you wouldn't."

Carly watched Simone deftly file her chipped nail. Nobody looked that gorgeous so early in the morning, she thought sourly. Simone looked as though she had spent ten hours in a beauty salon or, at the very least, had six people put her together. Carly was as green as Quincy's emerald feathers with jealousy. She forced a polite tone in her voice when she replied, "It's a little too early to leave yet. I have some work I have to do right now. If you like, you can wait, or you can go to the Cottage Inn and have some coffee."

"Coffee!" Simone said in a horrified voice. "Coffee is full of caffeine and it gives you pimples. I only drink herbal tea. I never touch a thing or put anything in my stomach that isn't one hundred percent organic. People are killing themselves with rich food full of all sorts of additives, and they don't even know it."

"Really," Carly said flatly.

"Just the other day I was talking to Judge Noble about it, and I told him I would like to do a once a week television show to bring all this to the public's attention. Vitamins are important. Natural vitamins. The judge is looking into the matter for me. If you stop to think about it, I'm the perfect person for the job. Look at my clear skin and eyes. I mean I really live what I talk about."

"Commendable," Carly muttered as she shuffled papers on her desk.

"I think I will go to the Cottage Inn. I always carry my own tea bags with me. Perhaps they'll be gracious enough to give me some boiled water."

Carly nodded. "I'm sure of it. You go along and I'll be ready when you get back."

Simone smiled and closed the door behind her. Carly sighed heavily as she pushed the papers in front of her into the wide middle drawer.

It annoyed Carly that Adam Noble's companion was going to be going along to inspect the house. Why? Was she going to live in it with Adam? Would she have final approval? Whatever the reason, it shouldn't be making a difference to Carly but it was. The plain simple fact of the matter was she didn't like Simone Maddox, and she was also jealous of Simone's relationship with Adam Noble.

If Melissa knew about this, she would stand over her and cluck her tongue in a motherly way and say, "Poor baby, poor Carly." She wasn't a poor baby and she wasn't poor Carly. She would handle this. She had momentarily let herself get sidetracked by Adam Noble's good looks and exciting attention. She didn't have to resort to snatching, or rather trying to snatch, a man from some other woman. She had merely daydreamed for a little while, but now her eyes were open and she would carry on—business as usual. Adam Noble and his friend were clients and that was all there was to it. Either she would make the sale or not. If not, Adam would go about his business and she would go about hers.

Carly's stomach lurched. If that was the way it was going to be, why did she feel this nauseous feeling in the pit of her stomach, and why was her heart fluttering like a trapped bird? Indigestion, she told herself, as she stuffed listing forms into her briefcase. That's what it was all right, she assured herself weakly, a good case of indigestion. A mint would cure it.

Promptly at nine-thirty Simone Maddox opened the door and waved to Carly. "I'm ready if you are."

"Come in. We'll go in my car to the dock. Will Rumley will be waiting on his launch to take us out to the island. That way we won't be hemmed in by the ferry schedule, if that's all right with you," Carly said coolly.

"That's fine with me," Simone answered just as coolly.

The trip to the island was made in silence, each girl intent on her own thoughts. From time to time Carly felt Simone's eyes boring into her and for some reason it pleased her. Was the beautiful woman concerned about Carly? Concerned that Adam might have some sort of feeling for her other than a professional one, or at worst, a mild flirtation.

Malcolm Sinclaire himself opened the door of the sprawling Tudor house. There was no other word for it but sprawling. Additions, Carly decided. Quickly, she explained why she was there so early in the morning.

"Well, I was thinking of listing the property with Clarence Olsen, but my wife seems to think his 'git up and go' got up and went. I don't think listing with your agency will be a problem. Seems to me my wife, Martha, belongs to some of the same clubs your mother does. Why don't you ladies take a look around and then we'll talk? We can have a brunch on the terrace if you have the time."

Carly smiled. She liked Malcolm Sinclaire immediately. And she knew he would give her the listing for the house. Melissa would go into orbit over it.

"Miss Maddox, why don't you take the upstairs and I'll stay down here? That way we won't influence each other with our comments." Simone nodded her agreement and immediately started up the long, winding staircase.

Malcolm Sinclaire whistled for a huge Irish setter and snapped a leash on the glossy animal. "Just make yourself at home. I'll just take this fellow for his morning walk and meet you back here on the terrace. If you have any questions, you can ask me then."

Carly wandered through the immaculately kept rooms on the ground floor. She realized the house was old, but it had been designed with an eye to the future. Tall, wide windows opened upon the incredible view outside the house. The front windows gave onto a sight of the sparkling blue bay, framed by tall, white birches. A gracious center hall was flanked on both sides by archways, each leading to a separate wing. On the right was a study-library, bookshelves climbing the oak paneled walls and surrounded by more windows. A room where even the pale, winter light would welcome you and encourage you to curl up on the chair nearest the Goliath fireplace to read. Underfoot, the floor was polished oak in a shade slightly darker than the walls, and it was covered with a rug of oriental design whose colors splashed and glowed in the streaming sunlight. Her eyes fell on the old-fashioned desk set between the two windows. Its dimensions were masculine, and its cherrywood gleamed from loving care. Instantly, a vision of Adam Noble sitting behind the desk flashed through her mind. She could almost see him, riffling through his papers and concentrating on a complicated law brief, only raising his head to smile at Carly as she brought him a cup of coffee. "This is insane," she muttered to herself. "I've got to stop thinking this way!"

Quickly, she hurried across the hall to the opposite wing. This was the front parlor, decorated with gentle Queen Anne furnishings. Like the library, its proportions were huge, and a view of the bay winked through the windows. Hearing Simone's footsteps upstairs, Carly hurried on to complete her tour. Behind the parlor was the dining room, complete with fireplace and tall, corner hutches displaying the family china. But it was the sunlight that beckoned through a doorway that drew her into the kitchen. As soon as she stepped over the threshold, she felt as though she was bathed in light. A skylight! And beneath it various pots containing local ferns and wild flowers. Long counters surrounded the perimeters and work area, and just beyond was a bay window, looking out onto the herb garden and the lawns. An old-fashioned table covered with a gay print cloth was nestled in a corner created by the window, and Carly couldn't think of a nicer place to have a morning cup of coffee. But beyond the breakfast area was another sitting room that backed onto the library. This, she decided, was her favorite room. Glass-paned doors opened onto a patio leading down to the lawns and the tennis courts. Just over the tops of hedges, Carly saw the striped awnings of the cabana in the pool area, its cheerful red and white vibrant against the blue sky.

Backtracking through the kitchen, bathed in the sunshine from the skylight, Carly admired the hanging ferns in their wicker baskets and the old-fashioned brick and copper utensils. The butcher-block countertops, real butcher-block not the plastic substitute, appeared to have been freshly scoured. Fragrant bundles of herbs, tied in small bundles and hanging from the beams, delighted her. It was a dream of a kitchen. Now she knew why Adam Noble adored this place.

So far, there had not been one negative thing about her tour. The house was exquisite and well kept. Even the slate floor she was standing on looked as though it had just been scrubbed. There was no dust, no sign of a cobweb anywhere. The asking price must be astronomical. Adam Noble could afford it, no doubt. Lord, what she wouldn't give to live in a house like this. She didn't know a soul in the whole world who had a fireplace in the kitchen, complete with hearthside rocking chair and yellow cat. Double ovens, double freezers and a monstrous refrigerator with double doors. Everything a cook could want. Everything a woman would want, right down to the oversized dishwasher. Any woman in her right mind would snap this up in a minute if she had any kind of sense at all. It was going to be interesting to see what Simone Maddox thought of the place.

Speak of the devil, she mused. "How quaint," Simone said walking through the swinging doors which led from the dining room into the kitchen.

"I'll go upstairs now and you can tour down here," Carly said shortly.

"Go ahead. Nothing up there impressed me one way or the other. It's just a bunch of rooms with wallpaper. I hate wallpaper. And it's so isolated! I don't see how anyone could live here. Little wonder the Sinclaires want to sell. This place must have driven her crazy!"

Carly stood for a moment at the foot of the circular stairway and tried to remember what it reminded her of. Tara in *Gone With the Wind*? Whatever, it certainly was elegant with the thick burgundy carpeting. She didn't know why she was tiptoeing through the rooms or why she felt the need to whisper. Each bedroom, and there were five, was perfection down to the last detail. Again, there was no dust, no sign of a cobweb anywhere. Mahogany floors! Unbelievable! Fireplaces in every bedroom! If she owned this house, she would never sell it. Never! This was a house for a family. A house to give birth in and a house to die in. It was the closest thing to perfection Carly had ever seen. And each bedroom had its own bathroom whose color scheme matched the bedroom. Gorgeous, simply gorgeous. It was suddenly important, paramount, that Adam see it with her. He loved this place; she could feel it, sense it. Now she understood what he was talking about. She had to get to him before Simone did. To Simone this was just a house. Adam Noble at some time in his life would make it a home. If Simone shared it with him, it would forever remain a house. She didn't know how she knew, she just knew.

Carly sat down gingerly in a high-backed chair and closed her eyes, pretending that she belonged in the house. A sudden, overwhelming possessiveness coursed through her. She would fight to the death for a house like this. She would work her fingers to the bone to keep it just the way it was. Dream on, Carly Andrews. If she worked her whole life, she could never afford a house like this one. Her mind started to race. Should she call Adam Noble from here before Simone could get to him and tell him she didn't care for the house? Should she wait? Just how much influence did Simone Maddox have over Adam Noble? She would wait till she got back to the office. As soon as she dropped Simone off at her car, she would make the call to Adam. Providing Malcolm Sinclaire didn't change his mind. Even if he listed with another agency, she could still show the house since the Andrews Agency was a member of the Multiple Listing System. Childishly, she crossed her fingers and then her ankles.

Carly glanced at her watch. She didn't want Simone spending too much time with Malcolm Sinclaire. God only knew what she would say or what kind of ideas she would plant in his head. Surely she knew about the bad feeling between Mr. Sinclaire and the Nobles.

Taking a deep breath Carly raced down the curving staircase just in time to see Malcolm Sinclaire walk through the French doors with the Irish setter.

"All finished?" he called, a smile on his face.

Carly laughed. "Mr. Sinclaire, this is the most beautiful, gorgeous house I have ever seen in my whole life. How can you bear to part with it? Who keeps it in such excellent condition?"

"Whoa, there young lady. One question at a time. I'm pleased that you like the house. It's been in the family for well over a hundred years. Martha is in frail health this past year, and the doctor recommended a warm climate, so we'll be going south. Our three married children live in the Carolinas and we want to be close to them and our grandchildren. We have a man and woman who come in every couple of days to dust up and straighten any mess Martha and I might make. Now, does that answer all of your questions?"

"I guess so. Your wife must love this house very much. I can't imagine a woman in the world who wouldn't want to live here. I think I might be tempted to sell my soul for this house if such a thing were possible."

Malcolm Sinclaire laughed. "It's timber and nails. A few doodads here and there for decoration. It's the people who live in a house that make it a home. I've been thinking while I walked my dog, and I have no objection to listing the house with you."

Carly smiled brightly. "Thank you, Mr. Sinclaire. If you're ready, I'd like to talk terms and join you for that brunch you were talking about."

"Good, good," Malcolm Sinclaire said rubbing his hands together. "I just heard Mrs. Nelson's car in the driveway. She went into town for groceries. She leaves the car at the pier and takes the launch in. She's our part-time housekeeper, and I'm sure if the right people bought this place, she might be persuaded to stay on and work the hours she's been giving us. We've had her for over twenty years. She's a gem, and Martha and I wouldn't be able to get along without her. Come along now, and we'll tell her we want something fattening for lunch. That's the best kind of lunch, and I only get away with it when Martha isn't at home." Carly laughed and agreed. What indeed could be better than a fattening lunch? Simone would probably go up in smoke or give a dissertation on organic foods.

Lunch turned out to be a delicious noodle and mushroom casserole with herbs and dripping in a buttery white sauce. A crisp watercress salad and iced tea accompanied it, to Simone's delight.

The moment Simone started her organic tirade, Malcolm Sinclaire squelched her by telling her he liked garbage and was a junk-food junkie for fifty years, and he had no intention of stopping, and he was seventy years old and who was she to tell him that he was dying a slow death and didn't even know it? Simone closed her mouth with a snap and then proceeded to nibble on the watercress like a rabbit.

Carly finished her lunch, and the second the table was cleared she opened her briefcase and withdrew the standard forms which required Malcolm Sinclaire's signature. They discussed mortgages and points and the ridiculous amounts of money people were asking for their properties. They finally settled on what Malcolm called a fair and equitable price, and he signed on the dotted line. They shook hands warmly and firmly.

Simone remained quiet on the walk to the dock where they met Will Rumley for the trip back to town. She didn't utter a single word, but sat back on her seat, her eyes closed as though asleep. It suited Carly just fine.

Chapter Six

A feeling of dread settled over Carly as she maneuvered the car through traffic. She didn't like Simone Maddox's silence. She should be making some comments on the house. Why was she being so quiet and why did her perfect jaw look so tight and grim? Was it possible that Simone was a "bright lights city girl" and the house on the island was too far from what she would consider civilization? True, you needed a power boat or had to use the ferry, but Adam Noble must have known that when he asked her to see about the house. Evidently, it made no real difference to him. Simone Maddox was another story entirely.

Carly fidgeted behind the wheel as she stopped for a red light. She had to say something, break the silence, so she had some idea of the beautiful girl's thoughts. Ammunition to defend her own liking of the Sinclaire property.

"Simone, what did you think of the house? Does your silence mean you didn't care for it?" Carly asked politely, dreading the answer.

Simone turned slightly in her seat and stared at Carly for a full minute before she replied. "As far as houses go, it was just another house. Personally, I prefer chrome and glass in the way of furniture. It was a little . . . woodsy for my taste, and of course, I detest the idea that you have to crawl into a boat to get on and off the island. The spray from the water makes my hair fall and my clothes damp. I don't think I would like having to wear a raincoat and carry an umbrella each time I wanted to go off somewhere. I don't think Adam will care for the place at all," she said coolly. Her eyes were veiled as she watched Carly for any reaction to her statement. Carly was not unaware of Simone's scrutiny, and her apprehension increased at Simone's cool words.

"Mr. Noble led me to believe this was exactly the sort of property he was looking for," Carly said quietly. "I'm sure I didn't misunderstand his instructions."

Simone tapped a long nail against her handbag as she continued to stare at Carly with veiled eyes. "Adam has a way of wanting something one day and forgetting about it the next. All of the Nobles are like that, but then I don't expect you travel in their circles so you really can't be expected to know how...how eccentric they are at times," Simone said knowledgeably.

A lump settled in Carly's stomach, and suddenly, she found it hard to breathe. She didn't believe a word Simone Maddox was saying. She wouldn't believe it until she heard Adam Noble say it. He wasn't indecisive. He had certainly given her the impression that he knew exactly what he wanted and would settle for nothing less. Adam Noble was a man who never "settled" as the saying went. Carly moistened her dry lips. She wouldn't have been that wrong in her judgment. Once she met him all her previous doubts concerning him and his family were swept away. Simone Maddox was wrong. Simone Maddox *had* to be wrong.

Carly parked the car behind the agency and climbed out. Simone waved and said, "Keep looking, I'm sure you'll turn up something that will appeal to *us.*" Not missing the emphasis on the word "us," Carly watched as Simone climbed behind the wheel of the small Mercedes and roared off down the street.

She had been dismissed like a school child. Carly fumed and admitted that it wasn't the curt dismissal but the word "us" that set her teeth on edge.

Angrily she unlocked the back door of the agency and made a beeline for the phone. "Adam Noble, please," she said breathlessly to the voice at the other end of the phone.

"Mr. Noble is away and won't be back until the weekend. Would you care to leave a message?"

Carly frowned. Four days. "Is there any way I can get in touch with Mr. Noble? This is Carly Andrews from Andrews Realty. It really is important that I speak with him as soon as possible."

"I'm sorry, Miss Andrews, but Mr. Noble did not leave a number where he could be reached. Perhaps I could have Miss Maddox return your call if the matter is urgent."

Carly felt drained. "No, that won't be necessary. Just tell Mr. Noble I called and that I found a property for him and that I would appreciate it if he contacted me as soon as possible."

"I'll take care of it, Miss Andrews," the impersonal voice responded.

"Thank you," Carly muttered as she hung up the phone. She drummed her fingers on the desk top. Why hadn't Simone mentioned that Adam was out of town? For that matter, why hadn't Adam told her he expected to be away for a few days? Carly's excitement over the Sinclaire property sank, taking her into the doldrums of uncertainty. The answer to that last question was easy enough. He hadn't told her because he hadn't cared enough to tell her. She meant nothing to him. Plain and simple. All that talk in the boathouse the night of the storm about how special she was. It was just another way of saying he didn't want her. To Adam Noble, Carly Andrews was just a means to an end. Perhaps he had heard a rumor that the Sinclaires were thinking of selling. He wanted that house out on Deer Island and she was in a position to know if and when it ever went on the market. The surprise was that the Sinclaires had decided to sell at this time. People like the Nobles always seemed to have things fall into their laps.

She had an obligation as a professional realtor. An obligation to the Sinclaires as well as to Adam. Carly determined that she would continue to try to contact Adam. For the moment there was little else she could do. After all, it wasn't as though a buyer for the high-priced estate would fall out of the sky.

Carly worked industriously for the balance of the week. Each day she called the Noble residence, leaving a message for Adam to return her calls. Each and every time except for the first call, Simone managed somehow to always pick up the phone.

When she called on Saturday morning, confident that Adam was home by now, Simone answered the phone again and informed her that Adam was sailing with his brothers. And yes, she would give him the message and have him get back to her. Carly waited all day in the office doing odd paperwork and when she ran out of chores, she gave herself a manicure. She had lunch sent in so she wouldn't miss his call. By four o'clock she was so edgy, she thought she would scream. She had to do something. Water the plants again that were already drowning. Clean the tiny-paned front door with Windex. She covered her typewriter, sharpened her pencils and put new refills in all the pens. The phone shrilled and she screamed at a friend to hang up because she was expecting an important phone call.

Excitement rose and ebbed like the tide in Carly's heart. One moment she imagined Adam's joy to find that the Sinclaire property could be his and then she believed that Adam did not really want the house after all. Suppose, which was more than likely, Simone already told him about the house. In which case, courtesy demanded that he at least call and tell her he wasn't interested.

The digital square on her wrist read five-forty. Who was fooling whom? Adam Noble wasn't going to call today or any other day for that matter. One more call. She would make one more call and then lock up and go home.

Carly dialed the now familiar number and waited. Simone Maddox answered, voice impatient. "I said I would give him the message and I have. He'll be in touch with you when he's free."

The connection was broken before Carly could do more than feel foolish.

"That does it," she muttered angrily. She bent over to remove her handbag from the desk drawer and then kicked the drawer shut with her foot. "You know what you can do, Mr. Noble, with your answering service. Well, I don't care if you don't want your 'dream house.' You can have some chrome and glass condominium with plastic plants for all I care. And you can eat TV dinners that Simone serves you straight from the microwave oven. You two deserve each other!"

At home, Quincy greeted the distraught Carly with a wild flapping of his wings.

"Knock it off, Quincy. I'm in no mood for your antics tonight. Some people have no consideration. Do things like professional courtesy count to rich people? Not on your life!"

Carly sat down at the table after she made herself a cup of instant coffee. Tomorrow was Sunday and on Sundays whenever the Noble clan was in town, they always gathered in the park, rain or shine for a game of touch football. She would make it her business to be an interested observer. If it was the only way she could get to Adam then that's exactly what she'd do. All she had to do was look in a copy of today's local paper to see what other clan the Nobles would be playing and the time would be listed. Sunday morning excitement! Ha! she snorted, scanning the newsprint. Her eyes flew down the columns.... Mrs. Nebit from Providence R. I. was visiting her niece, Barbara Smith...Cub Scout troop 77 was having a picnic at three o'clock...Mr. Hemple was in the hospital and receiving visitors now...Cathy Coolidge was vacationing in New York...the Hahn family had spent two weeks in the Great

Smokey Mountains...Mr. Olsen and his son John had caught a six foot 220 pound cod off Kennebunkport.... Here it is. The Noble Clan vs. the Conrads...Sunday 10 A.M.

That settled, it was time to think about dinner. Carly opened the freezer and withdrew a roast. She peeled off the wrapper, seasoned it and shoved it into the microwave oven. Quickly, she scrubbed some yams. Next, tossed a salad and then set the table. Melissa should be home soon. Should she tell her mother about Adam wanting the Sinclaire property or not? Carly decided she had enough problems without adding Melissa's questions to the list. Melissa would want to know where Adam had been, why he hadn't told Carly, etc., etc., etc. Besides, nothing was happening so why get Melissa's hopes up?

Her kitchen duties under control, Carly took her coffee cup and walked out to the backyard to sit down under the apple tree.

Melissa Andrews shook Carly's shoulder. "Wake up, Carly, dinner's ready. You look so tired, I really hated to wake you but that beautiful roast shouldn't be allowed to go to waste."

"I was just dozing, Mother. I'm starved. Do you believe I actually dozed off sitting here? I haven't done that since I was a kid."

"You must have been tired," Melissa said fondly as she ruffled Carly's dark curls. "By the way, I have a buyer for the Sinclaire property. An architect. It's just what he wants. I'm taking him to see it Monday afternoon. I called Martha Sinclaire this afternoon, and she said she would leave the keys with us on Monday. They're leaving for South Carolina so they won't be underfoot when the house is shown. That house won't be on the market long, I can tell you that. And what a commission! Carly, I'm so proud of you."

Carly's stomach lurched. An architect from New York. Of all the rotten luck. If there was anyone in the whole world who would appreciate the Sinclaire house, it was an architect. I could strangle you, Simone Maddox, she fumed silently.

Carly rinsed her hands and sat down at the kitchen table. Melissa chattered non-stop as she removed the roast and transferred it to a platter. "The price is right and Mr. Dillon will have no problem with the down payment or securing a mortgage. I haven't taken him out there but he knows the house. He visited there once when he came to Bar Harbor. It's almost as if he told me what he wanted as a prospective buyer and then the Sinclaires' house was put on the market."

Carly sliced into her yam with a vengeance. "Are...are...what did you say his name was? Oh, yes, Dillon. Is he here now?"

"He's been here for a week trying to get in touch with Clarence Olsen. He finally came to me just as I was closing up this afternoon. I must have come into the office right after you left." Carly toyed with the yam and then swished the salad around her plate. The rare roast beef she ignored completely. If she forced herself to chew, she would choke to death. This definitely wasn't the time to go on to her eternal reward. Not till she evened up the score with Simone Maddox.

Melissa ate ravenously, saying she only "wanted to pick" because she was gaining too much weight. "For God's sake, Carly, isn't it about time you threw that record out? I can't stand it another minute," Melissa said, throwing her hands up in the air. "Quincy," she bellowed to be heard above the stereo, "turn that thing off."

"What do you want from him, Mother, he's just a dumb bird."

"If he's smart enough to turn it on, he's smart enough to turn it off," Melissa said, attacking another slice of roast beef that she "picked" at.

The silence was deafening.

"You see? Now, if you could just train him to say the right thing at the right time, maybe we could palm him off on someone. I can't stand that bird, Carly. And to think that was all your father left either of us. He's getting a bit salty. Too much television. Curb him, Carly, before it's too late," Melissa said wiping at her mouth. "You do the dishes, dear. I'm playing canasta with the girls this evening and I want to change. My turn next week."

Carly set about clearing the table and straightening the kitchen. Her chores finished, she settled herself in front of the television to watch one ridiculous show after another until it was time to retire for the night. Tomorrow was another day. A day in which, with any luck, she would come in contact with Adam Noble.

Chapter Seven

Sunday turned out to be an overcast day with chiffon gray clouds threatening to erupt any moment. Carly felt as depressed as the day around her. She snuggled down into the raincoat she wore and watched as the Noble clan and the Conrads squared off for a rousing game of touch football.

Carly squinted. Where was Simone? Foolish question. She was no fool. There was no doubt in Carly's mind that the other woman was ensconced in the Noble mansion, nibbling on carrot sticks while Carly was standing around waiting for an audience with Adam.

Adam, where was Adam? All four Noble brothers looked alike in their jeans and ragtag college shirts. There he was. A perfect specimen of fitness. You could tell by his loose stance and the easy way he hefted the pigskin he was holding. She didn't remember his hands being so big, so powerful looking. Was he ever going to look toward the bleachers? Not likely. Right now, it was the Nobles and Harvard versus the Conrads and Yale.

Despite herself, Carly found that she was getting caught up in the game, silently rooting for the Nobles. They were athletes, there was no doubt about it.

Time was called and both teams walked to their respective places. Now, look toward the bleachers, Carly silently willed Adam. She stared intently, praying he would notice her and wave to show he knew she was there. He seemed oblivious to anyone but his family and friends.

Carly tilted her head. Of all the rotten luck, it was raining. Would the game continue? She waited as the few observers in the bleachers packed up their gear and raised their umbrellas. If they all left, she would have to leave, too. The rain was coming down harder and the crowd was now running toward their cars.

Carly stood and tightened the belt of her raincoat. She fished around in her bag for a scarf and tied it around her dark head. Morosely, she climbed down from the bleachers and started to run to her car. In her hurry to get out of the driving rain she stepped into a hole and fell face forward. Embarrassed, she struggled to her feet, wiping ineffectually at her mud and grass stained raincoat. She was soaked and mortified as she fumbled in her bag for the car keys. She felt like crying. Why was everything going wrong? Nothing she did was right any more. Nothing had been the same since she met Adam Noble. Her fingers found the metallic square the keys were attached to and she heaved a sigh of relief.

"One would almost think you were tired, from that mighty sigh," Adam Noble said, taking the keys from her and opening the car door. Carly gasped. How could he look so wonderful standing there in the rain with his hair plastered against his head? She smiled, fully expecting to see him return her effort. She sobered as she stared at the man. His eyes were cold and bleak, his jaw grim and tight. Even the knuckles of his hands were alabaster white as he clenched the door frame.

"Mr... Adam," Carly said shakily, "I've been trying to get in touch with you all week. I think I found..."

"Mr. Noble will do just fine, Miss Andrews. Messages! I've received no messages from you. As a matter of fact," he said coldly, "I've had Simone call your office practically on the hour to see what was going on with regard to the Sinclaire property. When Simone told me the house was for sale you could imagine my excitement. And now do you know what she told me? She said Kyle Dillon is in town and he has first dibs on the property. Kyle is an old college buddy of mine and he told Simone at a party last evening. Tell me, Miss Andrews, how did that happen? Never mind, I already know. Your agency is representing him, according to Mac Sinclaire. Somehow," he continued in his frozen voice, "I didn't think of you as a wheeler-dealer. Don't call me, Miss Andrews, I'll call you," Adam said stalking away, his back stiff and straight.

Carly was stunned. How had this all happened? She climbed from the car and ran after him. "Wait! You don't understand," she shouted, "It's not the way you think!"

What was the use? He couldn't or wouldn't listen with the rain pounding the way it was. Of all the miserable luck. She knew the minute she stepped from bed that it was going to be a bad day. "Nuts!" she shouted to be heard over the pelting rain as she sloshed her way back to the car. "Nuts to you, Adam Noble, and nuts to you Simone Maddox."

Carly tried to fit the key into the ignition with shaking hands. She succeeded on the fourth try as tears streamed down her cheeks. Why wasn't the stupid car starting? She turned the key again. Nothing. She waited and tried again. The battery. She had left her lights on somehow. She'd have to walk home. If she was lucky, she might get pneumonia and die and be put out of her misery.

The walk to the other side of town was an ordeal and Carly was exhausted when she opened the back door of her house. She kicked the door closed and then stepped out of her sodden shoes. "I hate him, he's insufferable, and that fast talking companion who answers his phone and delivers his messages. I hate liars and phonies, and Simone is all of those. And Adam's a bore and a conceited ass in the bargain. Who does he think he is anyway? A Noble. Noble Adam. Phooey," Carly shouted angrily.

"Carly is pretty mad," Quincy sputtered as he flew into his cage and perched on the swinging bar.

"One more word out of you and I'm cutting off your licorice supply," Carly yelled as she struggled to remove her sodden raincoat.

"Carly's a good girl," Quincy muttered as he taunted the drenched girl. "Quincy is a good boy. Quincy is a very good boy."

"That's not going to get you any licorice, so just shut up." Carly tossed a towel over the cage and peeled off her slacks and shirt in preparation of throwing them, along with her raincoat, into the dryer.

The phone in the kitchen shrilled. She reached out and placed the receiver next to her ear. "Carly Andrews," she said quietly.

"Miss Andrews, this is Simone Maddox. I've been trying to reach you for ever so long. I thought you must have gone out of town or something."

"Or something," Carly muttered, disliking Simone more by the minute.

"I can't tell you how upset Adam is over the fact that Kyle Dillon is trying to buy the Sinclaire property. He's getting ready to leave now for New York, and I did so want to try your number one more time, so I can tell him how you do business. Tsk, tsk, tsk, and to think you're one of the town's own daughters. After all the trouble Adam went to to steer you to the property. He's very distraught. I just thought I should bring it to your attention."

Carly listened with unbelieving ears. She couldn't be hearing this conversation right. She must be missing something somewhere. She'd been had! Simone Maddox was devious and sneaky. And there wasn't a thing Carly could do about it.

"Miss Maddox," she said sweetly. "I know exactly what you're up to, and I can't say I blame you. Adam Noble is a very attractive man and he does have pots of money. A very winning combination. I'm extremely flattered that you seem to think I'm some sort of threat to you. And before I hang up, let me say that I do wish you luck in getting your own television show. I can't wait to turn you on so I can turn you off." Carly slammed down the phone so hard, she thought she cracked the receiver. Quincy was right. Life was hell!

"You deserve a licorice stick, Quincy. Sometimes you're right," Carly said removing the towel and sticking a raspberry licorice stick in Quincy's beak.

"A wheeler-dealer!" Now that hurt. She had to defend herself somehow. After all, she did live and work in this town and she had a reputation to consider. Of all the dirty, rotten tricks.

Carly stomped about the kitchen, shivering in her underwear as she seethed and fumed. Briskly, she rubbed at her arms as goose bumps broke out all over her. Lord, she was freezing. A shower, she would take a shower and then get into bed till she warmed up. As if she could ever be warm again.

Quincy was up to his tricks again. What was he babbling about? Carly turned on the shower full blast, and at that precise moment a knock sounded on the back door. Quincy stared at Adam Noble through the back door and then flew out of the kitchen in search of Carly.

After a hastily eaten lunch that Monday afternoon, Carly was busily working at her desk, straightening out a contract for interested buyers. The slight tinkle of the bell over the door sounded, and it was a full moment before she could drag her thoughts away from the work before her until she looked up. There, standing before her, was a tall, muscularly built man staring down at her. For the moment little else about his physical appearance was communicated to her, so dazzled was she by his wide, ingenuous grin. In spite of herself Carly found she was smiling back and motioning him to have a seat opposite her desk.

A pearl gray Stetson hat was balanced on a knee. In a voice softened by the merest hint of a drawl, he said, "I'm Kyle Dillon. I have an appointment with Mrs. Andrews to see a house out near Straw Hill on Deer Island. I'm a little early, but where I come from a man never keeps a lady waiting. Our appointment was for two o'clock."

Carly's eyes flashed to the office clock. It was one fifty-nine. "I'm Carly Andrews, Mr. Dillon. Your appointment was with my mother. Right now she's in the back finishing her lunch. She'll be with you in a moment."

He was too big for the chair. All six feet of him and every inch of that rip cord muscle. Carly remembered her mother saying that Mr. Dillon was an architect. It hardly seemed possible that he could complete fine drawings with those big hands. Years of sun and wind were the only plausible explanation for his deep golden tan and the crinkles near his eyes told her he spent a lot of time laughing. She liked his deep chocolate eyes and the heavy fringe of lashes that any self-respecting girl would cry to have. He was a hunk, as the saying went, but the obvious humor in his face and his friendly attitude made Carly want to know him better in spite of the fact that he wanted to buy Adam's dream house. Considering Adam Noble's recent behavior, a girl should look out for herself. She definitely did not owe Adam Noble a thing.

"My mother told me you were from New York but your accent . . ."

"Ma'am, I'm from Dallas, Texas. I've been hanging my hat in New York for a while because I've been finishing up a job for a friend of mine. I'll be heading back to Texas just as soon as I check out this property to see my folks. I hope to live here six months of the year if things work out the way I plan. Now, tell me about you. What's a pretty girl like you doing hiding her light under a bushel in Bar Harbor? You look as though you were made for bright lights and the busy city."

Carly laughed. "I do like the bright lights of the city. I go into New York every so often to see some plays and check out the restaurants and do some Fifth Avenue shopping. But I always come back here, this is my home."

"I can relate to that, Ma'am." Kyle smiled.

"Mr. Dillon," Melissa Andrews said, walking into the room, "how nice to meet you at last. I see you've met my daughter. You're right on time. I like that in a man. Shows responsibility."

"I've been getting acquainted with Miss Andrews. You have a nice office here," Kyle said, looking at the window frames. "Sturdy building, built to last. Not like some of those cracker boxes I've seen at the other end of town. If there's one thing that will curl my lip, it's tract houses. I know, I know," he said holding up his hand at Melissa who was about to protest. "Someone has to design and build them because folks need places to live. I accept it, but I don't like it."

"Carly, call her Carly, everyone else does," Melissa said with a calculating look in her eye.

Carly winced. She could almost read Melissa's mind. Super jock, pots of money, lucrative profession that he took seriously and easy on the eye. Was he ever. She felt a giggle work its way up her throat and quickly suppressed it. She knew what was coming next even before Melissa spoke. So did Kyle Dillon from the look on his face. It was obvious that he liked the idea.

"Darling Carly, I just remembered that I have to take a spin out to see Daphne Winters. There's something wrong with the mortgage and her lawyer wants to see me. Why don't you be a real love and take Mr. Dillon out to the Sinclaire property for me? I peeked into your engagement book, and your afternoon is free. By the way," Melissa chirped, "are you by any chance going to the fish fry at the Bradshaw's?"

Kyle Dillon laughed. "You bet, I'm the guest of honor it seems. I've just finished a job for Mr. Bradshaw's new office building in Bangor. What about you two pretty ladies, are you going to be there?"

"I'm not, I have a political rally to attend, but Carly is going, aren't you darling?"

"Mother, you're about as transparent as cellophane. Yes, Mr. Dillon, I was invited, and yes, I'm attending."

"Then perhaps you'll allow me to escort you. I'd like to get to know you better while I'm here."

Carly's heart fell to her shoes. How could she refuse this charming, eligible man? She couldn't. But, what was it going to do to her plans to seek out Adam Noble? Would Adam be there? Of course he would be there, even if he had to fly back from New York just for the fish fry. When the Bradshaws threw a fish fry, the whole state turned out, it seemed. It was rather like a command performance and one Carly was sure Simone Maddox wouldn't want to miss.

"That sounds...fine," Carly said quietly, to her mother's obvious approval.

"It's settled then. You're my date for the evening. You'll have to take me in hand—I'm just a poor little old country boy and not used to all of this razzle-dazzle."

Carly returned his grin. "Off the top of my head, Mr. Dillon, I'd say you were doing just fine. Everyone knows poor little old country boys grow up into dashing, handsome men who can handle anything."

"That's probably the nicest thing anyone has said to me in a long time." Kyle grinned, showing square, white teeth.

Melissa tossed the key ring to Carly who caught it deftly. "I guess we might as well be on our way then," Carly said quietly. Why was she feeling so disloyal? Why did she feel she was doing something sneaky by taking Kyle Dillon out to the Sinclaire property? She had done all that was humanly possible as far as Adam Noble was concerned. A man's arms really could make you a prisoner and soft, passionate kisses could make you lose all perspective just as the romantic novels said. She shouldn't be thinking of that now. For now, she had to concentrate on Kyle Dillon by keeping up her end of the conversation and always remembering the business at hand.

Kyle turned out to be an easy conversationalist as they made the trip to the island. For the most part Carly listened and was surprised at how easy it was to be with this good-looking man. And the best part was he didn't have a Simone Maddox on his arm, and from the things he said there wasn't anyone like her in his background. No one was going to take this man down the garden path. Both of his feet were on the ground and his head, while pretty far up, was definitely not in the clouds. Straightforward and honest. Two of the most important traits in a man. And he had a delightful sense of humor. A winner. Then why did she feel as though she had lost something? Finding no answers, Carly smiled and linked her arm through Kyle's as they made their way up the path leading to the Sinclaire house.

"Carly, I've seen houses and I've seen houses. But this is one for the books. I'll buy it right now."

"But you haven't even seen the inside," Carly said forlornly.

"I don't have to. I know what I'm going to find when I get in there."

She shouldn't be feeling so dejected, so lost. Kyle's face wore a look of absolute rapture as he moved to view the house from different angles. He loved the house. Mr. and Mrs. Sinclaire would be pleased to sell this man their home. He loved it and would grow to love it more each day. Carly knew that in sight of six months the property would cease to be referred to as the Sinclaire property. He would make his presence known and felt, and it would be the Dillon property over on the island. Not the Noble property but the Dillon place. She choked a little as they continued toward the house.

If only his enthusiasm weren't so contagious. In spite of herself Carly was caught up in Kyle's delight over the small estate.

"I've been through the house, so I'll open the doors for you and you take the tour yourself. Browse and wander to your heart's content. I'll sit out here under the birch trees and think pleasant thoughts."

"Never mind the pleasant thoughts," Kyle said exuberantly. "Start the paper work. By the time we get back to the office I'll have the check ready and I'll sign on ye olde dotted line."

Carly's heart plummeted to her shoes. It was settled. She had no other choice. She couldn't stall, even if she wanted to. It wasn't fair to Kyle.

A long time later Kyle Dillon joined Carly under the birch trees. "This place is the closest thing to perfection I could ever hope to find," he said reverently. "There's little to change, little to fix. It's a small piece of paradise."

Carly gulped. It was definite now. Even if she had a faint, dim hope in the back of her mind, it was gone now. It was his, Kyle Dillon's house. The only thing that would hinder the sale now was the terms, and she knew that this man would sell his soul, leave no stone unturned, to get this property.

"I'm glad you like it," was all she could manage.

"Like it! Carly, I would give up everything I hold dear for this place. This is the kind of place that grabs you in the gut and never lets go. It's perfect for raising kids. Course, it needs a woman. But," he grinned, "one thing at a time. I want to live in this house, get to know it, and let it get to know me before I start thinking about things like sharing it with some woman." For the first time he seemed to notice Carly's quietness. "Is something wrong? Did I say something out of turn? Sometimes I can get carried away. I should think you'd be happy making a sale of this sort. Your agency should get a really nice commission off this."

"No, nothing's wrong," Carly forced a smile to her face. "Late night last night, guess I'm a little tired," she fibbed.

Kyle accepted her explanation totally. "What I don't understand," he said, lacing his sun-darkened hands across his knees, "is why no one else snapped up this property. The asking price is high but worth every penny. There's a lot of wealthy people around here and it doesn't make sense. Is there something you aren't telling me that I should know about this property?" There was a hint of concern in the big man's voice as he asked the question.

Carly quickly reassured him. "Of course not. The house was just officially listed and only went on the market. I did have a prospective buyer for the place. As a matter of fact, he was the one who steered me to the property and I managed to get the listing. Once I listed it I tried for a week to get hold of the man. None of my calls were returned."

Kyle laughed. "His loss is my gain and I can't say I'm disappointed. Is it someone from around here?"

"Yes, Adam Noble," Carly said quietly.

"Adam! You aren't kidding me are you?" Kyle asked in amazement. Not bothering to wait for a reply, he continued. "I went to college with Adam. We played football together and were on the same wrestling team. He's a nice guy. He's really going to be bent out of shape when he hears I beat him to the draw. That guy was always fast on his feet. And all because he didn't return phone calls.'' Kyle chuckled, a delighted, smug look on his face.

Carly didn't want to hear any more. Of all the rotten luck. By tomorrow everyone in town would know Kyle Dillon was buying the Sinclaire property. Adam would be at the fish fry along with Kyle. Carly groaned inwardly. And to make matters worse, she was Kyle's date. When you reached bottom, there was no place to go but back up. What she had to do now was act as though she hadn't done anything wrong. And she hadn't. It wasn't her fault. A pity Kyle's friend, Adam Noble, wouldn't look at it that way. She didn't have to feel defensive and on the brink of disaster. It was a straightforward business deal. There hadn't been any double-dealing. Now, why had that phrase entered her mind? Because, she answered herself, that's what Adam Noble is going to think. Maybe she could plead a headache, the office would burn down, Quincy would get sick. Anything, so she wouldn't have to go to the party.

Coward! she rebelled. You didn't do anything, so why do you have to hide and pretend you did? Everyone is aboveboard.

"I hate to leave here. I could just sit here all day and stare at that house," Kyle said contentedly. "However, I have to get back, and the sooner I sign the papers, the sooner I'll feel as though I own this chunk of paradise. What do you say, pretty lady, are you ready to leave?"

Carly grinned. It was hard to stay depressed around Kyle Dillon. "As ready as I'll ever be. I love this place too. It's so...so...perfect is the only word I can think of. If I owned this place, I would never part with it. It's the kind of house that goes with big families and down through generations. You're very fortunate that you can afford it, Kyle."

"Pretty lady, I'd work the rest of my life digging ditches if I had to for this house. I can feel it, it's part of me already. I'd never give it up."

"It looks like you won't have to as long as you meet the requirements," Carly smiled. "I think it's safe to say the Sinclaire property is yours."

"That's the second nicest thing I've heard in a long time," Kyle grinned, touching her cheek softly with the tip of his finger. Embarrassed by this little gesture of intimacy, Carly lowered her eyes, suddenly standing. Even before his arms came around her, holding her close to him, she had expected his embrace. And before his head lowered and his lips touched hers, she had known he would kiss her. And even before she had experienced that light caress, she had known he would be tender and gentle. Why then didn't her heart leap and why didn't she feel herself lost in the world of his arms? And why was she allowing his kiss a second time? Deeper, more demanding. It was a salve to her wounded pride. Had Adam wounded her so deeply that she needed to find solace and peace even if it meant turning to another man's arms? Whatever her reasons, she allowed it, wanted it.

At last Kyle Dillon broke away from the embrace. The expression on his face when he looked down at her was gentle and happy. Silently, he took her hand in his and led her to the quay where their launch was waiting.

Chapter Eight

Melissa Andrews danced around the office the moment the door closed behind Kyle Dillon. "Do you know what the commission on that property is? If we don't sell a house for the next year, we're still in the black. Congratulations, Carly, you did a super job of selling the property," Melissa said enthusiastically.

"Mother, the property sold itself. I didn't have to open my mouth. He saw, he liked, he bought."

"Be that as it may," Melissa said airily, "I prefer to think of you as a super salesman, excuse me, salesperson. And, Carly, tomorrow at the party, Adam Noble and Kyle Dillon, and one of them is your date. I'm so proud of you. You know, Carly," she lowered her voice to a bare whisper, "if you played your cards right, you could play one against the other and who knows? Adam showed a great deal of interest in you before he left. What happened? You might come up with a winner after all. It's time for you to think seriously of getting married. You don't want to be an old maid, do you?"

"Mother, don't help. And for your information, Adam Noble is spoken for. Remember the beauty who trails after him?"

"See, see, you've given up already." Melissa pouted. "But you do have a point whether you realize it or not. She trails after him, there is a very big difference. And," she said loftily, "there's no ring on her finger so that makes anything else more than fair."

"Mother, please. I can do it myself. If I feel like it, that is," Carly said hastily.

"So far time has been just crawling or marching by, Carly. At your age it speeds up and literally races. If you get married, you can have Quincy."

"Mother, stop helping, and bribery in the form of Quincy is definitely no inducement. Any self-respecting man would run the other way if he found out I came with an interfering mother and tart-tongued parrot who is addicted to raspberry licorice sticks."

"Oh, Carly. You're just being difficult."

She wasn't being difficult; she just wanted to be left alone to ponder the day's happenings and what might happen tomorrow. She felt weak in the knees and her elbows hung limply, like a Raggedy Ann doll, just remembering the feel of Kyle Dillon's arms. And the feel of his lips on hers. Delicious was the only word she could come up with. Her heart had fluttered like a wild bird when Kyle kissed her. She had been content when he released her from his embrace. Was that what she wanted, contentment? Was that what love was? Contentment would sooner or later turn to boredom. She had heard that often enough from aunts and girl friends who had gotten married right after school.

Adam Noble's embrace had been different. He had been masterful the way he drew her into his arms and held her prisoner. Her heart had literally pounded in her chest and her senses reeled till she thought she would faint. And the feel of his lips, gentle, yet demanding. And when he released her she was sorry, she wanted more, so much more. Had she been wrong, did Adam Noble's eyes promise more or was she deluding herself with wishful thinking?

She was getting a headache. Time to go home. Dwelling on the new man in her life and another who had entered and exited too quickly was not going to do a thing for her splitting head. Two aspirins and a hot shower might cure the ache in her head, but what about her heart?

"Darling," Melissa trilled, "I have a marvelous idea, stupendous, actually. What do you say to both of us going to the Chanticleer Chateau for dinner? My treat. We both deserve a rest from that microwave oven. We won't even have to go home to change. All either of us needs is a little fresh makeup and you could use a touch of color at the neck. Here," she said whipping a gossamer melon scarf from her hand bag.

Carly shrugged. This was one of those times when it didn't pay to argue with Melissa and she did have a certain light in her eye. Why not? At least she would be spared a few hours in front of the boob tube. "All right, Mother, let me freshen up, and you're right about the scarf. Is it new?"

"Oh, Carly, I've been wearing it for months now. We'll really celebrate tonight. Let's get the works, surf and turf, and a magnificent dessert. We will throw caution to the winds and gorge to our hearts' delight. I deserve it," she said airily. "All week, I eat those dietetic killers and I really deserve this. So do you, darling. Tonight is ours. We'll hoot with the owls."

"If you hoot with the owls, you won't be able to soar with the eagles in the morning," Carly called tartly over her shoulder on the way to the powder room.

"Darling, I do not soar...ever. I glide, there is a difference," Melissa called to Carly's retreating back.

Melissa was at her best when she was going public and the Chanticleer was definitely public. Carly ordered white wine for herself and a Martini, extra dry, for her mother.

"Darling, brighten up, this is a happy occasion, and remember, it's tax deductible," Melissa said as she rearranged the table accompaniments to suit herself.

"I should have known," Carly groaned.

"Known what? Oh, look, Carly, there's Mr. Dillon at the bar. I thought he said he was going home? Should we ask him to join us? Carly, are you listening to me? Carly, as a mother, I feel I should say something. Mr. Dillon is a fascinating man. Now, as your mother, I wish to apprise you of something you overlooked. Mr. Dillon is a man of today. Do you know what I mean?"

Carly gulped at the wine and centered her gaze on her mother. "I'm not sure. Don't play cupid, Mother, I'm too old and so are you."

Melissa's face took on a maternal glow that she usually reserved for Christmas morning. "Darling, Mr. Dillon is a today man. His plans and ideals are for the present. Men like Kyle Dillon rarely build toward the future. I know what I'm talking about. It's not that he isn't steady or dependable, he is. He has things to do and places to go. He's an idea man who makes things happen. Today in Maine, tomorrow in Beirut. Do you understand what I'm saying?"

"Perfectly." And she did. "Mother, I just sold the man a piece of property. I have no intention of losing my heart to Mr. Dillon." How true, Carly thought. She couldn't lose her heart when she had already lost it to Adam Noble.

"Now, you take Adam Noble. Adam is a man of tomorrow. Adam knows where he's coming from and where he's going. His aims are set on the future. A girl couldn't do much better than Adam Noble. And it doesn't hurt to remember that Adam comes with gilt-edged securities."

"That does help, doesn't it?" Carly's sarcasm was wasted on Melissa who was waving her long arm in the direction of the bar.

"Be charming, Carly. Mr. Dillon is coming over here. Let's be hospitable and invite him to dinner. Charming, Carly, with a capital C," Melissa warned.

"Why not? It's tax deductible!" Again her sarcasm was lost on Melissa who was showering Kyle Dillon with her hundred-watt smile. In spite of herself Carly smiled too. How could she be angry with Melissa?

"Mr. Dillon, what a pleasant surprise. Join us, please. We haven't ordered yet."

"If you're sure you wouldn't mind," Kyle said looking directly at Carly.

The words were forced but Carly managed to get them past her tongue. "By all means, Mr. Dillon, join us."

"This is some kind of restaurant," Kyle drawled as he looked around the elegant dining room. His tone as well as his gaze was approving.

"It is the best restaurant around unless you want to go all the way into Bangor. It's a quiet night, but on weekends you need a reservation and then you wait at least an hour for a table. We like it, don't we, Carly?"

"Very much," Carly replied.

"I don't want either of you ladies to think I hang out in bars. It's just that I've been on a high since leaving your office and the Bradshaws are out for the evening. I was sort of left to fend for myself. Now I'm glad that I decided not to go to Bangor with them."

In spite of herself, Carly laughed at his winsome tone. He was putting Melissa on and she was eating it up, or was she?

"I'll join you on one condition." Carly and Melissa waited expectantly for the tall man to make his condition known. "That you allow me to pick up the check."

"I wouldn't hear of it," Melissa demurred. "After all, we did invite you."

"I insist," Kyle said firmly.

"I never argue with a man who insists." Melissa capitulated. "I do so love forceful men. My husband was like that—forceful and dynamic."

Carly almost choked on her drink. The only forceful thing her father had ever done was inherit Quincy, over Melissa's protests, and the only dynamic thing he had done was to marry Melissa. Douglas Andrews had been a scholar and a dreamer, a man of a thousand years ago, and Carly had loved him blindly, as had Melissa. If

Melissa preferred to remember him as forceful and dynamic, so be it.

"I'm sorry I never got to meet him."

"I am too, Mr. Dillon, I am too." And then Carly understood. It was Melissa's way of pointing out to Carly that her earlier statements concerning Kyle Dillon were true. He was a today man, her father was a man of yesterday. Dreamers. Adam Noble was a man of tomorrow and all the tomorrows beyond today.

"Tell me, Mr. Dillon..."

"Please, call me Kyle. Mr. Dillon is my father," Kyle interjected.

Melissa nodded. "Tell me, Kyle, how do you like Maine? Have you met any of our town fathers since you've been here?"

"Actually, I've been here many times. I used to come here on semester breaks with a friend of mine while I was in college. I spent a summer here my second year of college."

Melissa's eyes narrowed slightly. "Anyone we know?" she asked casually.

"Adam Noble and his family. Adam and I were roommates back in college."

"Really," Melissa said coolly. "Have you seen the Nobles since you've been here?"

"Not really. I called the manse several times and was told that Adam was out of town. I left my number, but he hasn't returned my calls. I wanted to see the judge before I left. We used to have some really rousing chess games. They're wonderful people. They opened their home to me and treated me as though I was one of their own. Hospitality like that I don't forget. Adam came with me to Texas on several Christmas vacations. He never could get the hang of riding a horse. Old Adam, he beat me out of everything but that. Just couldn't come to terms with a four-legged beast."

"What do you mean, he beat you out at everything?" Melissa asked softly.

"Well, Ma'am, Adam was always the best in everything. He didn't even have to work at it, it just came naturally. Book learning was a snap, sports were a natural, and when it came to the girls, well, Ma'am, they knew a winning combination when they saw it. I hear he's thinking of running for state senator, is that true?"

"As far as I know it is. He was born to politics as were all his family."

"I think you're right," Kyle said thoughtfully. "Senator, governor and, who knows, the White House. Anything is possible."

"What about you, Kyle, what are your plans for the future?" Carly asked.

"Right now, I have no plans beyond settling in to my new house once you ladies give me the right of way."

There was a tinge of anxiety in Carly's voice when she spoke. "You've definitely made up your mind then, this is the house you want?"

"Pretty lady, I signed those papers with just that thought in mind. I still can't believe that house is going to be mine."

I can top that, Carly thought, I can't believe it either and I'm the one who sold it to him.

"I think it's time to order," Melissa said reaching for a menu the waiter was holding out to her. "I recommend the surf and turf, Kyle."

They gave their order and ordered another round of drinks.

Drinks wound their way into dinner and then dessert. Kyle proved to be not only an amusing dinner companion but a knowledgeable one. Carly enjoyed herself as did Melissa.

"Darling," Melissa said, addressing herself to her daughter. "Would you mind if I skipped dessert and joined the Zacharys? See, there they are over in the corner of the room. Adele hasn't been feeling up to par and I've been meaning to stop by and check on her. This is my chance. I'm sure neither of you young people will mind. Thank you for dinner, Kyle. You must permit Carly and myself to cook you a home-cooked dinner before you leave. We have this fantastic microwave oven which just does everything you tell it to do."

"I'd like that very much, Mrs. Andrews," Kyle said, rising to hold out Melissa's chair. Melissa nodded graciously as she wafted to the far corner of the room.

"I like your mother," Kyle said sincerely.

"I sort of like her myself. She doesn't exactly fit into the ordinary garden variety of mother, but I don't think I would want her any other way." Carly smiled.

"I can understand that. When I left for college, my dad took me aside and sort of whispered to me. What he was trying to tell me was to remember to write home to my mother and then he said, 'Son, your mother is the best friend you'll ever have.' He was right and I've never forgotten those words."

"I think I agree with your father, Kyle."

"You take Adam Noble now, his mother died when he was young and he was raised by his father and a whole parcel of maids and live-in help. Of course, there's all those brothers and sisters of his, but no one can make up for a mother. Adam took to my mother and she took to him. She always said Adam was a man, even when he was a young college student. She said I was a boy compared to him. I don't mind though, Mom is usually right."

Carly stared at the man across from her. He did mind; he minded terribly. She could sense it. Adam was a man and this tall person across from her was also a man in a different way, a man who lived and savored the present. How astute of Melissa to have seen it so quickly.

"Well, what shall we have for dessert?" Kyle asked, opening the menu.

"I think I'll pass."

"I was hoping you would say that. I don't think I could eat another bite. What do you say we take a nice long walk and work off all the damage that we've done?"

Carly straightened the scarf on her neck and picked up her handbag in preparation to leaving.

"Would you look at that!" Kyle exclaimed. Carly followed Kyle's gaze and swallowed hard. Adam Noble and Simone Maddox were making their way to the table. Even from this distance Adam's face wore a chiseled, cold, hard look. The word granite came to Carly's mind. It was too late now to try to tell him and explain how Kyle had won the Sinclaire property. Please don't invite them to sit down; please, she prayed silently as Kyle and Adam went through the back slapping routine that is so common to men.

"I would ask you to join us, but we were just leaving," Kyle said amiably. "You know Miss Andrews, don't you, Adam?"

The reply, when it came, was chips of ice carved from an iceberg. "Very well, as a matter of fact. You've met Simone, haven't you?"

"At a dinner party last week and before that two years ago in Monte Carlo, right?" Kyle grinned. "Don't you remember, Adam?"

"*You* remembered!" Simone trilled delightedly.

Darn. Two years ago in Monte Carlo! That meant Adam and Simone were a thing, an item, as the saying went. Two whole years! Carly's heart thudded sickeningly. She had to get out of here and fast before her emotions got the best of her. How gorgeous she was, how sophisticated. And the burnt orange caftan that would look like a rag on anyone else was perfection on the stunning Simone. Evidently Kyle thought so, too, the way he was ogling her.

"Miss Andrews, how nice to see you again." Simone's tone and the look in her eye clearly stated something else. Carly nodded, not trusting herself to speak. Instead she gave the melon scarf another hitch and stood up, not bothering to wait for someone to hold her chair.

"I'm ready when you are," Carly said coolly to Kyle, ignoring Adam Noble and his beautiful companion.

Carly walked around the side of the table and inadvertently brushed against Adam. When she realized how close she was to the man, she turned and stumbled. Strong arms caught her and held her the barest fraction of a second. Just long enough for Carly to stare deeply into the coldest eyes she had ever seen in her life.

"Are you all right, Carly?" Kyle asked with concern as he placed a firm, hard grip on Carly's trembling arm. "C'mon, let's get on with our walk. I feel all that drawn butter settling around my waistline, not to mention a whole loaf of garlic bread. Funny how the salad and the vegetables seem to go to your feet and everything else goes to the waist."

"It does seem that way," Carly smilingly agreed.

The walk, while not lengthy, was enjoyable. Carly strolled hand in hand with Kyle pointing out various points of interest to the architect's amusement. "I really think we should be getting back. Tomorrow is a work day for me and I want to be bright-eyed to do all the paperwork on the Sinclaire property," Carly said as an inducement to being taken home. Everything was such an effort. I should be enjoying myself and I am, to a degree. I just want to go home and think about Adam in the privacy and darkness of my room.

"Whatever you say, Carly. I really enjoyed this evening. I hope you did too."

Carly's face wore a stricken look. Had she been that obvious? No, he was just making conversation. "Of course, I enjoyed it. You're a very easy person to be with. And I do want to thank you for dinner."

"It was my pleasure and I'd like to do it again, soon, real soon."

"I'm not hard to find." Carly smiled warmly.

The ride back to her house was pleasant with the car windows open and the soft music coming from the stereo system in the mile-long Cadillac. Kyle walked her to the door and waited while she fumbled with her key.

Carly's head and heart raced as if each were vying for the winning place. Please don't try to kiss me, please don't try, she repeated over and over to herself.

The door open, Carly turned to face Kyle who had backed off a step. "Good night, pretty lady. I'll be calling you." Without another word he turned on his heel and walked down the driveway to his waiting car.

Somehow Carly managed to get through the night and the following day. Always her thoughts were on Adam. Melissa suggested they close the agency early so Carly could get a head start on getting ready for the Bradshaw's fish fry.

"Darling, you need scent from the skin out—bubble bath, bath oil, and then spray your entire body with the scent. You want to waft. Waft, Carly, as you move about. Scent is so important. It teases men. If you use a fragrance that is 'you,' anytime a man smells it he'll think of you even if it's being worn by some voluptuous femme fatale. Carly, you aren't paying attention," Melissa said irritably.

"Mother, stop helping," Carly said just as irritably. If there was one thing she didn't need right now, it was an observer while she dressed for the party. She resigned herself to Melissa's presence, spraying lavishly of the intoxicating scent.

"Good, perfect," Melissa chortled. "Now show me what you're wearing. Oh, Carly, you can't wear that! Don't you have something a little more . . . that shows off some skin . . . ?"

"Mother, I'm not being auctioned off. What's wrong with this sun dress?"

Melissa pouted. "Nothing. Absolutely nothing, if you were going to a tenth-grade spring dance with a freckle-faced boy. I didn't realize they were still using dimity. It's tacky, Carly, and it won't do." Her voice was firm and held a no-nonsense ring to it. Carly trotted back to the closet and frowned.

Melissa tapped her foot impatiently as she watched her daughter move hangers in the large walk-in closet. "You irritate me beyond belief, Carly. You knew this party was coming up weeks ago. You also knew you would be attending and you should have been prepared."

"I was prepared till you started helping me. You should have told me I was a side of beef you wanted to sell off to the highest bidder," Carly snapped.

"You're an ungrateful daughter," Melissa retorted amiably. "I'm leaving. I know when I'm not needed. You just go right ahead and wear whatever tacky outfit that pleases you. I've done my best," she said dusting her hands together and exiting the room.

Carly heaved a sigh of relief. Now she could get on with her picking and choosing. Melissa was usually right. She did have a flair for fashion and what was right for special occasions. Just because it was a fish fry didn't mean the affair was casual dress. In fact, the Bradshaw affairs usually stopped just short of white tie and tails. She finally selected a sleeveless plum-colored silk dress, slit up both sides. The deep V of the neck should please even Melissa. Simple, elegant, and if the designer label meant anything, she would be as well turned out as Simone Maddox. The sexy three-inch heels with the two slim braids of leather across her toes would definitely add, not detract from the overall effect. No jewelry except the tiny gold and diamond earrings and the diamond snowflake on her hand. Necklaces and bracelets were a no-no as far as she was concerned. What with the high price of gold, every woman there would be dripping in the stuff. If one of them managed to fall into the pool, she would go straight to the bottom. Now in her opinion, *that* was tacky.

Quincy flew into the room and was immediately attracted to the brilliant baubles in Carly's ears. "Carly's a bad girl," he said lighting on her shoulder, picking at the stones with his hooked beak.

"The only way you're going to get the fix you need, and by that I mean your daily quota of licorice, is to say that Carly is the most beautiful, the most ravishing, the most sexy girl in the world. You say that and you can have two sticks of licorice." Carly grinned as she tried to apply a light dusting of eye shadow to her upper lids.

The emerald bird ignored her as he zeroed in on her flashing finger as Carly's hand moved from the eye shadow to her eye. "Say it, you dumb bird, say that Carly is the most beautiful, the most ravishing, the most sexy girl in the whole world."

"Life is hell! War is hell!" the parrot cackled excitedly.

"You just might have a point at that." Carly giggled.

Carly stood back to survey her handiwork and was satisfied. She wasn't a Simone Maddox but she could definitely hold her own. "And, I even have a brain. What do you think of that, Quincy?"

"Let me see how you look," Melissa said, coming into the room. "My goodness, Carly, you do look..." she searched for the right word, "ravishing. Yes, you really look quite stunning," Melissa said sincerely as she watched her daughter twirl around for her benefit.

"Thank you for your help." Carly grinned. "Well, time to go. Are you certain you won't come along with me instead of the Zacharys? We can still call them and tell them of your change of plans."

"No, darling, I'll go to the fish fry with the Zacharys as planned. And what's more, I'll stay completely out of your way. That dress doesn't signify having a girl's mother hovering in the background."

Carly let out a sigh. "Okay, Mummy dearest, you'll see me... when you see me."

The party was off to a good start with people milling companionably about. Drinks and hors d'oeuvres on large silver trays were circulating on the shoulders of trim waiters in red jackets. The tantalizing aroma of lobster boiling in huge caldrons at the end of the terrace drew the crowd for inspection. Carly made chatter with old friends and clients she had done business with, all the while searching for some sign of Adam Noble. He was nowhere in evidence, nor was Simone. No matter where she moved or who she talked with, the topic of conversation was Kyle Dillon and his purchase of the Sinclaire property. A new man on the scene, and from the looks of things, a rich and successful one. Eligible bachelors were hard to come by in Bar Harbor.

She knew Adam and Simone had arrived an hour later when all heads turned toward the entrance. Heads always turned for the beautiful people. She was no different. She stared as did the others at the delightfully outrageous gown Simone wore that stopped just short of being obscene. All that good, clean living, Carly thought tartly as she gazed at the dress that was parted to the waist. She drew in her breath. Simone did have a beautiful figure. The dress was so simple it had to cost a king's ransom. And Adam, so casual in his suit of white linen which showed off his marvelous coppery tan. They looked like the perfect couple. They were the perfect couple. Carly winced slightly as she watched Simone link her arm possessively in Adam's and smile winningly at those around her. Her small maneuver clearly said to the men she was taken, and to any woman who might have faint ideas of capturing Adam, it meant "Hands off!"

Any man who could be maneuvered that easily wasn't worth it, Carly told herself as she smiled up at Kyle Dillon.

"He hasn't changed at all." Kyle grinned. "Wherever Adam Noble was or is, you can count on finding the most beautiful woman. They look perfectly matched."

"You sound as though you're discussing two pedigree bloodlines," Carly muttered.

Kyle frowned. He would never understand women. He raised an eyebrow in question at Carly's sudden anger but said nothing.

"You don't like Simone, do you?"

"I don't like her and I don't dislike her. Let's just say she's not one of my favorite people."

"Another logical answer. Tell me, Carly, could I ever be one of your favorite people?"

There was an intensity in the tall man's face that unnerved Carly. "I don't know, Kyle," she said, opting for honesty. No game playing for her.

Kyle took her by the arm and led her to the buffet table. "Now, let's have some frivolous party conversation."

"Oh, I do love frivolous conversation." Carly laughed, the infectious sound making those around the table smile. "You look so...so winsome and sort of wispy. It goes with frivolous conversation." Carly continued to laugh.

"I've been called a lot of things in my day but never wispy and winsome," Kyle said in mock anger. "Is it becoming on me?" he demanded.

"Quite," a cool voice answered. "It looks like our climate up here is agreeing with you."

Carly watched as the two men shook hands and then backed off a pace almost as if they were squaring off. They had been friends at one time, that was obvious, but now there was a strain. It was evident to Carly in Kyle's stiff back and in Adam Noble's narrowed gaze.

"I hear talk that you're going to run for state senator. You were born to politics. Didn't I always say you had the makings of the consummate politician?"

"That's what you said, all right," Adam said coolly. "I hear you're the famous architect who is designing the multi-billion dollar airport terminal on the West Coast."

"I don't know about the famous part, but I'm the one doing the designing. Adam, I can't tell you what a challenge it is. My moment of glory, so to speak."

Carly waited, hardly daring to breathe. Where was Simone? Out of the corner of her eye she saw a flash of tangerine silk and sighed. She was being well taken care of by a bevy of men with stupid looks on their faces. When were they going to mention the Sinclaire house? When was Adam going to acknowledge her presence? The tension between the two men was so thick she thought she would suffocate. Say it, say something, her mind ordered. No, more inane party conversation.

"How long will you be here, Kyle? I'd like to have you over to the house. I know the judge would like to see you. He's been following your career for the past several years." Adam's tone was cordial but still cool. Carly sensed that while he offered the invitation, he was hoping Kyle would turn it down.

"I called the house several times but was told you were out of town. I'm afraid I won't be able to take you up on it now. Give the judge my regards. To answer your question, I expect to be here another week or so before heading west. I have a little business to take care of and my hosts have plans for me or so they said. And this little lady here," he said placing his arm around Carly's shoulders, "is hopefully going to take up the slack and entertain me a little."

Adam stared at her, his eyes shards of ice. His mouth was a grim, tight line and Carly could see the stiff set of his shoulders. She smiled happily and thought she would explode with the effort it cost her. All she wanted to do was throw herself into Adam Noble's arms and tell him everything was a mistake. She wanted him to smother her with kisses and hold her in his arms and say it didn't matter, that he was going to make everything right. That's what she wanted.

If Adam Noble was experiencing any emotions, and if Carly was interpreting them correctly, all he wanted to do was strangle her. She couldn't remember ever seeing such hostility emanating from an individual before. Emanating from him and directed at her. Things are tough all over, Mr. Noble, Carly thought nastily. Why should she be subjected to the man's hostility? She had done her job and more if the truth were known. It wasn't her fault if Simone Maddox had a rope around his neck and had named herself his protector. If the delectable Simone wanted to run interference for Adam Noble, it was no concern of hers. Just say one word to me, Adam Noble, just one word, and I'll let you have it with both barrels.

Kyle noticed for the second time the hostility Adam was exuding and correctly surmised that the petite creature next to him was the reason. He grinned down at Carly and then winked. She smiled up at him and suggested in a husky whisper that they walk in the garden. As far as she was concerned, Adam Noble had been dismissed.

With a last scathing look in Carly's direction Adam headed toward the knot of men that surrounded the tangerine-clad figure of Simone Maddox.

"I hate tangerines. They're always sour and full of pits," Carly blurted to Kyle.

"I always thought they were sweet but kind of tangy. When I was a kid, I looked forward to getting them around Christmas."

"They're sour and full of pits. Take my word for it," Carly replied firmly.

Kyle grinned when he noticed the direction her gaze was taking. Come to think of it, he had had a sour one or two. His face continued to wear an amused expression as he led Carly to the garden.

"And where do you think you're going?" a shrill voice demanded. Kyle and Carly stopped in their tracks before Midge Bradshaw raised her voice a second time. "Carly," she continued to shrill, "release this man immediately! I want to show him off to the other guests. Later, you can have him."

Kyle raised his eyebrows and followed the tall heavyset form of Midge Bradshaw. "Don't worry, Carly, I'll find you if I have to set out with Midge's spaniels to track you down."

"You go along. I'll wait in the garden. Go ahead, I'll be fine, really. See, I have a drink and everything. I'll wait for you by the birch grove."

Carly sat for a long time with her untasted drink getting warmer by the moment. She kicked her shoes off and curled her feet under her on the soft chaise. It was so peaceful here in the darkness with the sounds of the party going full swing. She was dozing, on the brink of sleep, with the plastic tumbler about to slip from her hand. In her twilight sleep she felt the glass being removed from her limp hand. Kyle must have done his duty and come to find her. "I hate tangerines," she muttered.

"I never liked them myself, too many pits," replied a cool voice.

Carly was up off the chaise like a shot. "Who... what..."

"Your Lochinvar is over there with the ladies," Adam pointed toward a cluster of people at the far end of the pool. "I'm leaving now, but I couldn't go without telling you what I thought of your business practices. I've heard of scalping, but your tricks are about the most blatant I've ever seen used around here. You knew how much I wanted that property. I spilled my guts to you and this is how you repay me, by putting someone else onto the Sinclaire property. I trusted you to act on my behalf and you repay me by double-dealing with a friend of mine."

"Now, just a darn minute, Adam Noble..." Carly sputtered.

"No. Not another minute. I thought you were honest, that you had integrity and I hoped that you might..."

Carly didn't give him a chance to finish whatever he was about to say. Her eyes spewed fire as she stood to her full height, aware her spike heeled shoes were somewhere in the grass. "Look, Mr. Noble, if you want to attack me, Carly Andrews, that's fine. I'm sure I don't come anywhere close to that tangerine you had hanging on your arm. That's okay, I accept that. Don't you dare, don't you ever dare attack my business methods. I called your home every day, sometimes twice and left messages for you to call me. I did everything I could to make sure you got that property. Kyle Dillon had left messages for you and you didn't seem to get them either. Why is it so unlikely that my messages were lost? Don't talk to me about business ethics. Take it up with that orange ball over there. And another thing, don't you ever speak to me again. Do you hear me? Not ever!" Tears glistened in her eyes as she bent to find her shoes. The dew on the freshly trimmed grass shimmered in the dim light from the Chinese lanterns but it was also slippery and she slid and nearly fell.

Strong arms reached for her and held her close. "Never is such a long time."

"Never is forever," Carly stated hotly. "I thought I told you never to speak to me again."

"That's what you said all right," Adam said as he brought his mouth closer to hers. "Is that what you really want?"

His wine-scented breath teased her senses as she fought with her emotions. The heady fragrance of his after-shave lotion made her head spin. What did she want? Who cared. Right now, all she wanted was to surrender to this powerful force that was holding her a prisoner. An invisible devil perched himself on her shoulder and she pulled away. "Do you really hate tangerines?"

"With a passion," Adam replied huskily. "Is there something about fruit you can't deal with, something I should know?" he teased as he bent his head again toward her mouth.

Carly moved even closer. "I can think of at least one other thing I would rather discuss right now," she murmured as his lips found hers.

Neither Carly nor Adam saw Kyle Dillon on the edge of the birch grove. They didn't see his shoulders slump, and if they had, it wouldn't have made a difference. They were one, lost in their moment of eternity.

Carly was shaken to her very toes with the intensity of the long kiss. Adam gently removed her from the circle of his arms and stared down at her, his face expressionless in the dim lantern light. He should be saying something, Carly thought wildly. How could he kiss her and hold her the way he had and not say something? What was wrong; why was he suddenly acting so...so indifferent? Did he think she went from man to man, kissing and then telling? Say something, don't look at me like that, she pleaded silently.

Adam's face remained inscrutable and he stared a moment longer before he walked away from her. Carly had never felt so alone in her life. Tears of frustration and longing rolled down her cheeks as she searched for her shoes. She couldn't put them on now, her feet were soaking wet from the dew on the grass. The best thing she could do now was make her way through the birch grove to the parking area and go home. I must have some invisible mark on me that says, "dump on Carly, she won't mind." Well, Carly did mind and Carly was angry. Angry at Adam Noble and angry with herself. And, yes, she was even angry with Kyle Dillon. Where was he? He had left her to go with Midge over two hours ago. The angry tears continued to roll unchecked down her cheeks as she made her way on bare feet to the parking lot. By the time she pulled into the driveway and parked behind Melissa's car the salty droplets were reduced to a mere trickle.

She was a wishy-washy female. And fickle as they come. She fell into his arms as though he were some warrior returning from slaying all the bad dragons of the world. How could he just leave her standing there with her heart in her eyes? In her bare feet no less, like some street urchin. How dare he kiss her like that! Who did he think he was anyway?

"Toy with my affections, will you?" she muttered angrily as she slammed the refrigerator door shut, deciding there was nothing worth eating, nothing that would make her less angry with the tall, handsome man. And that...that...blueprint fanatic, where was he? He hadn't even shown up. Two hours he had left her in the birch grove! What did he think she was supposed to do for two whole hours? The word date must mean something else in Texas, Carly fumed as she stalked around the kitchen. Men! Put them in a paper bag, shake it up and they all came out the same. Male chauvinists, the lot of them. She didn't have to put up with either one of them. She was, after all, her own person, always had been.

Why was she tearing herself apart like this? Neither Adam Noble nor Kyle Dillon were worth the effort. Anything that caused this much emotional turmoil should be eliminated. How dare they treat her in such a shabby fashion!

She stomped up the stairs and down the hall to her room. Several hours later, Carly had just slipped her nightgown over her head when Melissa walked into the room. "Home so early?" she yawned elaborately. "Carly! What is that suitcase doing on your bed?" she demanded, now completely awake.

"I'm not running away, I'm just going someplace," Carly replied through clenched teeth.

"I'm glad to hear it. Would you mind telling me where you're going and why? And what makes you think I would think you're running away?"

"Well, I'm not, so there. Don't help, Mother. I can take care of this myself."

"I can see that for myself. You must be planning on spending a lot of time in bed wherever you're going."

"No, I'm not going to spend a lot of time in bed. In fact, I may never sleep again. Why did you say that?" Carly asked as she continued to toss garments helter-skelter into her suitcase.

"So far," Melissa said ticking off items on her fingers, "you packed three pairs of pajamas, four nightgowns, two robes and three pairs of slippers. How's that for starters?" She yawned again and perched herself on the arm of a slipper chair covered in lavender velvet.

Carly looked baffled for a moment but quickly recovered. "I'm trying to decide which ones to take. I'll sort through later. This is just angry packing," she said defensively.

"I understand that perfectly," Melissa said nonchalantly. "Now, would you tell me why you're angry? So angry that you're running away, excuse me, going away?"

"I really don't want to talk about it. And don't think you're foisting that bird off on me either. Where I'm going, they don't allow birds."

"Fine. Fine. Where are you going? I'm your mother. I have a perfect right to ask that question and a perfect right to expect some kind of an answer. Carly, this isn't like you at all! You've always been so...so stable. I'm the flighty one. You always had your feet on the ground. Dependable, if you know what I mean. This is so entirely out of character for you that I don't understand."

"Dump on me too! Why not? Why should my own mother be expected to understand? Just dump on Carly, she won't mind. She's stable, dependable, and you can always count on her having her feet planted firmly on the ground. Well, let me tell you something. I'm tired of being stable and dependable. I only wanted to stick my head in the clouds and soar a little. I did that and look what happened to me," Carly blurted. "You know I have feelings and emotions just like everyone else. I hurt. I'm vulnerable. Why can't people see that? Why do I always have to be trampled on? What makes me different?"

Melissa was at a loss. "Carly, baby, tell me what happened. I don't know if I can help, but I'm here for whatever good I am."

"Oh, Mom," Carly sobbed throwing herself into Melissa's arms. "I goofed it all up and I was left high and dry, as the saying goes." She sniffed and dried her eyes on the sleeve of her nightgown. "I'm okay. We'll talk in the morning, okay? I just want to get into bed for now. Go to bed, Mom, I'm okay."

"If that's what you want, Carly," Melissa said, patting her daughter affectionately on the head. "If you need me or decide you want to talk, call me." She left the room in a swish, leaving in her wake the faint, elusive scent of night-blooming jasmine.

Carly slid beneath the covers and then pulled them up to her chin. She felt like sleeping with the light on. She didn't want to lie in the dark and imagine even darker thoughts. She slept eventually, her dreams filled with visions of herself mailing one letter after another, all the while listening for the phone to ring.

Carly woke exhausted when the alarm shrilled the start of a new day. Her head throbbed and her shoulders ached. Maybe she was coming down with the flu or some kind of virus. Come to think of it, she was overdue. She had gone through the entire winter without one case of the sniffles. She was getting sick, and if you were sick, you got to stay in bed. When you stayed in bed, you didn't have to go to work and see people. You didn't have to put on a brave front or make decisions. When you were sick, you got waited on hand and foot; your every need was seen to by someone else. The last thought was the one that made her slide from the bed. She could just see Melissa tying a thermos of hot tea around Quincy's neck for him to deliver because she didn't want to climb the steps. "It was a thought," she muttered to herself as she headed for the bathroom and her morning shower.

Stepping back into her room, she noticed the open suitcase on the floor at the foot of her bed. That was exactly what she should do. Go away somewhere, get her mind off the whole Sinclaire mess. Somewhere there was plenty of life and lots of diversion. New York.

Satisfied with her decision, she dressed with care and then quickly packed her bag and overnight case. She called the airline and charged a round-trip ticket on her American Express card. Now all she had to do was have some breakfast, give Quincy his licorice stick, kiss Melissa goodbye and take off.

Chapter Nine

By using superhuman effort Carly managed to while away two full weeks in the Big Apple. She stayed with her friend Jenny from college, alternating her time between shopping, luncheons with old friends, and partaking occasionally of an intimate dinner with still older boyfriends who professed they were glad to see her and asked how long would she be in town. She gave vague answers to what she thought was their obvious relief. She was past tense in more ways than one. She might as well go home. She had wanted to get Adam Noble out of her system and it wasn't working. You can't run away from your problems, she told herself over and over as she packed her bag for the return to Bar Harbor.

She had run away when she left Melissa two weeks before. In her heart of hearts she knew the only reason she chose New York as her destination was that she hoped in some way she would be walking down the street and accidentally bump into Adam Noble. It always happened that way in the movies and the place was always New York City. It was time to go home and she hadn't seen Adam at all.

Carly glanced at her watch. She still had time if she really wanted to see Adam. She could even delay her flight till tomorrow morning if she had a mind to. Chez Martine. That was where Adam said he did his gourmet cooking on weekends. This was the weekend. Why not? She had told him she was going to try out the restaurant when she got to New York again. Why not tonight? Why not indeed? But Adam had said he catered private parties. Well, there was only one way to find out and that was to go the restaurant. Before she could change her mind, Carly pulled out the heavy Manhattan directory and riffled through the pages. Chez Martine, East 52nd Street, between First and Second Avenues. All she needed was a taxi and some money.

The square black phone on the tiny table in the foyer drew her eye. Perhaps she should call for a reservation. And while she was at the phone, she might as well call the airline and change her reservation for the following morning.

"Chez Martine," a warm, friendly voice with a hint of a foreign accent announced.

"I'd like to make a reservation, please."

"Your name please, and how many in your party?"

"Carly Andrews. I'll be dining alone."

"And what time would you like your reservation?"

Carly glanced at her watch. Thirty minutes by cab at the most. "Eight o'clock will be fine."

"Your reservation is confirmed, Miss Andrews. Thank you for calling Chez Martine."

Carly looked at the phone as she replaced the receiver in the cradle. She dreaded the thought of eating alone in a popular New York restaurant especially at the height of the dinner hour that was a usual hour for dinner dating. Much as she hated the feeling of being conspicuous she would suffer through the experience in the hopes that she would see Adam Noble. For an instant her heart fell. Maybe Adam wouldn't be there. Perhaps she was planning all this for nothing.

Refusing to face that possibility, she made a quick call to the airline and her plane reservation was changed and rebooked by an obliging computer. Now all she had to do was open her suitcase and take out one of the new dresses she had bought during one of her shopping sprees.

An hour later Carly was dressed in a raspberry silk dress and ready to go. She looked pretty and for the first time in two weeks she felt pretty, more like the Carly Andrews of old. Amazing what the thought of seeing the man in your life could do for your spirits. There was no point in denying, even to herself, that she was in love with Adam Noble. For all the good it's going to do me, she thought unhappily as she climbed into the rear seat of a Checker Cab.

It was a basement restaurant, like so many in the city, and from the appearance, it was one that catered to intimate dining. It would be dim with the candles on the tables and there would be romantic couples seated in nooks surrounded by foliage. Her stomach started to churn as she opened the door and walked into the dimly-lit room that held a large, circular bar. She blinked and tried to focus her eyes.

The hostess was tall and model-thin. She made her way to Carly smiling a welcome. It seemed to

Carly that all eyes were on her as she was motioned toward a tall podium holding an open reservation book. "Name please."

"Carly Andrews. I'm dining alone." Now why had she said that? Any fool could see that she was alone. Carly tried to stifle her defensiveness. She was here in this place eating alone by her own choice. If she felt out of place and conspicuous that was her own problem, no one else's.

"This way please." Carly followed the hostess and wondered fleetingly how she could stay so thin and work in a restaurant.

"Here you are," the hostess said, indicating a tiny table set back in a dark corner of the room. It was next to the kitchen and beside the dish and utensil counter.

She had read in several women's magazines that restaurants as a general policy seated solitary diners somewhere off to the side. This was especially true if the solitary diner was a woman. For the moment, she was grateful. The table's proximity to the kitchen was just what she wanted and it would also serve to make her feel less conspicuous.

The wine list was brought and Carly scanned it quickly, ordering the house white wine. A glass carafe was placed before her and the amenable waiter poured her the first glass. He held out a menu in a heavy burgundy folder with a long golden tassel dangling at the end. Carly again scanned the printed words, trying to decide what to order.

"If I may make a suggestion," the waiter said softly. "Chez Martine is most fortunate to have on the weekends a fabulous chef. Today his specialty is Osso Bucco à l'orange and roulade de veau Florentin."

He was here, in the kitchen. Adam Noble was really here. Out there, just beyond the door, only yards away. "Fine, the Florentin please," she decided, her eyes straying to the kitchen door. Whatever it was she was sure she would love it.

Carly's meal arrived and was served to her with what she could only call reverence. It was apparent that Adam's reputation as a chef was held with great respect even with the waiters.

She was aghast at the huge platter of food the waiter was placing in front of her. Even though she was hungry and eager to taste Adam's cuisine she couldn't possibly make a dent in the amount served to her. The New England Patriots Football team combined with the Boston Bruins hockey team would have been hard pressed to eat what was on the platter. She glanced in askance at the waiter who suddenly seemed decidedly uncomfortable. She risked another glance, this time around the room. The other diners seemed to have normal portions.

Another quick glance at the waiter and Carly saw he was smiling in the direction of the kitchen door. Turning, she caught sight of Adam's laughing face looking back at her through the round glass window. Within a split second, he was gone.

Adam Noble was trying to make a fool of her, embarrassing her in front of the other patrons. Trying to remain calm, she waited for the waiter to serve her a portion of the veal on her plate. Instead, and looking quite uncomfortable about it, he removed her service plate and placed the huge platter in front of her. Squelching down the urge to get up and run away, Carly instead picked up her fork and tasted the tempting dish. The delicious food stuck in her throat and tasted like sawdust to her palate. She knew the food was expertly prepared but somehow she had great difficulty swallowing it. Adam had purposely set out to make her feel foolish. Well, she would treat him in kind.

She raised her index finger slightly and the waiter appeared as if by magic. Carly moistened her lips and motioned for him to lean closer. In a voice barely above a whisper she said, "I really hate to complain but this is overspiced and overdone. Please return it to the chef and ask him to make me a salad. Lemon dressing, please."

The waiter blanched. "You . . . you want me to take all of this back . . . and . . ."

"Yes. I do," Carly said simply, her tone soft, ladylike and yet authoritative.

"Yes, a salad. Lemon dressing." Solemnly, he removed the huge platter from the table and made his way into the kitchen.

She sat there resolutely, little quivers of apprehension dancing through her veins. She told herself she should pay her bill and leave. Now. Before the waiter relayed her criticisms to Adam. The sound of an angry crash reverberated through the room and its source was the kitchen. Again Carly wished she had the courage to get up and leave before Adam himself came into the dining room to strangle her. She knew he took an artist's pride in his culinary techniques.

Again the waiter returned, looking shaken and harried. He placed the salad before her. Suddenly, Adam himself appeared opposite her and seated himself at the table. "You ordered it, now eat it. And to set the matter straight, the veal was neither overspiced nor overdone. Do you understand?"

"Perfectly, Mr. Noble. You're telling me it's perfectly all right for you to criticize my business practices but it isn't all right for me to do the same."

Adam ignored her words. "Eat," was all he said.

Carly was about to obey him when something inside her rebelled. She signaled to the waiter and asked for her check. The poor hapless man looked first at Adam and then at Carly.

"You're beautiful when you're angry," Adam said quietly. "You're always beautiful. Apologize to me for your comments concerning my food."

"Apologize!" she gasped, hating the smile that was already forming on her lips. "Do you really think I'm beautiful?"

"Of course you are. You might operate your business a little on the shady side but you're still beautiful. Apologize."

"No. You apologize to me for what you said about my business ethics."

"Impossible," came the sharp reply.

Carly looked at the nervous waiter. "My check, please."

"I'll take care of it," Adam offered, "it's the least I can do seeing how dissatisfied you were with the meal." He fixed his indigo eyes on her and the flame from the candlelight seemed to burn within them. He was angry, terribly angry, Carly could see it in the tight set of his jaw and his unblinking gaze.

Gathering her purse and scarf she hastily stood up, wanting only to get away from Adam, away from Chez Martine, before she burst into tears. How could he be so unbending? Did he think it was only by pure chance that she had come to Chez Martine? Couldn't he see that it had only been to see him again, hopefully to patch up the misunderstanding between them?

Literally running from the restaurant, she found herself wandering aimlessly down the street, knowing she shouldn't be walking alone at this time of night but not caring. How could she love such an obstinate single-minded person the way she loved Adam? Regardless of how she could, she did love him. And now, nothing would ever come of it. For whatever it had been it was over.

A car pulled alongside of her and the door opened. "Get in," was the curt order. "You really should know better than to wander around alone at this time of night."

Adam's voice was stern, sharp. Carly obeyed, never considering to do otherwise. Her heart beat in sudden raps against her rib cage. Folding herself into the sports car she had no sooner slammed the door shut when he spun away from the curb. In the close confines of the car her shoulder was almost touching his and daring a glance at his stony profile and tightly set mouth that conveyed his anger, she drew closer to the door.

"Where to?" Adam asked curtly.

"Aren't you supposed to be on duty at the restaurant?" she asked in turn.

"Everything is prepared—they only have to serve it. Where to?"

Carly gave him the address and leaned back in her seat. She stared straight ahead, not daring a second look in his direction, not wanting to witness his anger. From time to time she felt rather than saw him turn in her direction; felt his gaze piercing her. She felt confused, neither knowing what to do or what to say. They continued to ride in silence and Carly thought her heart would break. She wanted that gentle, attentive, easy-to-be-with Adam she had come to know in Bar Harbor before the situation with the Sinclaire property had erupted.

The car came to a smooth stop at the curb outside Jenny's apartment house. "Thank you for the ride," Carly muttered.

"My pleasure," was the abrupt reply.

"I'm sorry," she whispered.

"It's late, Miss Andrews, you'd better get inside. I'll wait here until I see that you're safely indoors." His voice was flat, nearly as emotionless as the expression on his face.

It was all she could do to whisper a husky, "Good night Adam." Had she been mistaken or had he said, "Good night, Carly"? And his voice had seemed soft, void of annoyance.

She would never know for certain because she had already begun to slam the door shut when he answered and she couldn't bring herself to open it again on the chance she had been wrong.

Almost the instant the outside apartment door closed behind her she heard the sound of his car pulling away; the powerful sound of the engine drowning out her stricken sob.

Desolate, inconsolable, she pressed her face against the glass pane and stared out into the night. "Good night, Adam," she whispered again. "Goodbye."

Chapter Ten

The next morning Carly lay quietly in bed in the guest room of Jenny's apartment, listening as her hostess readied herself for an early tennis date. Jenny had been marvelous. Instinctively, she had included Carly in some of her plans, taking her out, introducing her to new people, but Jenny had also realized that Carly had a need to be alone some of the time and this was graciously allowed. Much as Carly was fond of Jenny, she couldn't face her this morning. If Jenny should return from her tennis date before Carly left for the airport, their goodbyes would be said then. If not, the free and easy Jenny wouldn't be upset by a phone call from Bar Harbor.

Carly rolled over on her side, appreciating the quiet of the cozy guest room. Her cheek felt hot against the pillow as she recalled the evening before in the restaurant with Adam. Misery, misery! Why couldn't she be as cool as a cucumber and carry things off the way other women seemed to do? All poise and stature. Oh no, not good old Carly. No, she was all big feet and trembling fingers.

Outside her closed door Carly heard Jenny whisper a faint "Good morning" and "I'll see you later after tennis." Carly couldn't bring herself to answer, preferring that Jenny think she was still asleep. After the snick of the lock hitting home on the front door sounded, Carly reluctantly threw back the covers and planted her feet firmly on the floor. She couldn't allow herself to lie abed and hide from the world. After all, truth to tell, it was really only Adam Noble that she wanted to hide from. Outside her window were the muffled sounds of light traffic. Saturday morning in New York City was a place of slowed paces and gleeful shopping. Business had ceased for the week and, wonder of wonders, it was almost possible to get a cab just by standing on a corner and waving an indecisive finger. Not like during the rest of the week when you practically had to throw yourself into the rush of traffic and pray the cab would stop before it ran over you.

After brushing her teeth and running a brush through her crackling dark hair, she padded out to the minuscule kitchen in search of a cup of coffee. The electric percolator hissed quietly and puffed out fragrant streams of brew. When she found the milk in the fridge, it was well on its way to sour. Sighing, Carly poured herself a mug of coffee, added an ice cube to cool it down, and sipped carefully. It tasted flat without the milk. Just as flat as the rest of her life would be without Adam Noble to sweeten it. Grimacing at the thought, yet unconsciously squaring her shoulders for courage, she pushed the thought aside and went into the expansive living room to peer out into the street.

A sporty black Corvette screeched to a halt in front of the apartment building and, even as she watched, Adam Noble unfolded his lean length from behind the wheel.

Adam! Here! What did he want? She wouldn't open the door. She would pretend that she'd already left for home. There was no way he could know that she was still in Jenny's apartment, hiding like a child from the bogeyman. There was no way on earth that she was going to open that door. No way!

Trembling, Carly moved toward her bedroom, the furthest place away from the front door. She would stay there until he went away. Then she would get her gear together and take a cab to the airport. He'd never find her, never again. She would hide, hide away from Adam Noble. Hide, and the rest of her life would be dark and without light. The light from Adam's smile.

Suddenly Carly stopped, frozen, thoughts rolling, heart pounding. No! She was through hiding. She couldn't hide for the rest of her life. Sooner or later she would have to face him, and now was as good a time as any.

Brazenly, she stalked back toward the front door. She ran a peremptory hand through her hair and tightened the belt of her robe. Swinging open the front door, she stood against it, prepared for battle, relishing the thought of it. For once and for all, she was going to take Adam Noble head on.

The sound of the buzzer sounded through the apartment. Steeling her voice to keep it from quivering, she answered the ancient intercom.

"Yes?" she answered into the small microphone.

"Carly? That you? It's me, Adam." Was that a note of uncertainty she heard in his voice? Was it possible that the stalwart Mr. Noble was actually uneasy about his uninvited visit?

"Yes?" she answered again; this time with more confidence.

"I want to see you. Can I come up?"

Carly's finger hesitated over the electronic button that would unlock the door downstairs and admit him. Deliberately, she punched her finger onto the button. A few seconds later she heard the rapid sound of his steps on the stairs. When he at last rounded the landing, he found her leaning against the door jamb, arms folded across her chest, an expression of resignation on her face.

"Morning!" he said brightly, ignoring the thinly veiled hostility in her eyes.

Carly nodded, knowing that if she spoke her voice would waver and crack and once again he would have her at a disadvantage.

"Smells like coffee. Could I have some?" The boyish smile that touched his lips and lighted his eyes sent a pang of tenderness through her heart. No, she must stop this. Adam Noble was not a little boy begging for a cookie. He was a grown man who was very much in control of seeing his needs and desires filled. Instantly, she remembered the feel of his lips against hers, the way his arms enfolded her, keeping her for his own, protecting her from the world.

Before she lost her control and allowed him to see the vulnerability in her eyes, she turned her back and walked to the kitchen, hearing him enter the apartment and close the door behind him.

She had expected him to wait for her in the living room, so when she turned to the counter where the electric percolator steamed, she was shocked and unnerved to find him standing close behind her.

"Do you always do that?" she asked, annoyed.

"Do what?"

"Creep up on women that way."

"Only when they're as lovely as you and have the morning roses on their cheeks." He gazed down at her, captivating her with the ingenuousness of his smile.

"And do you always think a woman is going to fall for that line of blarney?"

"Most times," he said softly. "Especially when it's true."

"Well, not this woman!" Carly warned. Abruptly, she turned her back on him and poured the dark brew into a mug, filling another for herself.

Taking the mug from her, he winked conspiratorially. "Ah, the first hemlock of the day. Smells delicious. Did you make it?"

"No, I didn't make it. And if you've come to remind me what a fool I made of myself last night, you just may be wishing that *was* poison in that mug."

The look he gave her was startled, shocked and surprised that she would even think of him being so ungentlemanly. Carly had to hand it to Adam. Whatever the situation, he would charm his way out of it.

"Adam, did anyone ever tell you that your career in politics would be brilliant?" She had meant it as a gibe, but he took it seriously.

"As a matter of fact, yes. But it's always nice to hear it."

Together they laughed, enjoying the teasing and the unusual form of camaraderie they shared.

After several sips of coffee, Carly turned to him again. "Suppose you tell me just why you are here?"

"To take you home."

"Home! I've already made airline reservations."

"Cancel."

"I couldn't do that. I had intended to be home by late this afternoon and that's just what I'm going to do."

"Cancel. Please?" The honesty of his gaze penetrated Carly's determination.

"Why? It seems senseless to drive all the way to Bar Harbor. That's almost an eight hour trip. I could be there by plane in a little over an hour...."

"Stop fighting it, Carly. I want to spend some time with you. It's been a long time...cancel," he ended with authority as though he weren't used to having his requests and decisions ignored.

For a long moment Carly found herself looking into his eyes, questioning the expression she found there. That he was perfectly serious was evident. "Adam...really, my reservations have been confirmed. I was planning on returning to Bar Harbor yesterday, only..." Instantly, she realized she had given herself away. Now he knew that she had put off returning to Maine in order to seek him out at the restaurant. Angry with herself, Carly heard herself say, "You're just looking for someone to keep you company on the drive home. I'm as good as anyone, is that it?"

"Wrong." He frowned.

"Why don't you get Simone to fly down to New York? She'd be more than happy to drive all the way back to Maine with you and have you all to herself." As soon as she uttered the words, she realized how juvenile they sounded. She had to stop herself from clamping her hands over her mouth. Now he knew about her jealousy.

"If I wanted Simone, she would be with me right this very moment and I wouldn't be standing here scuffing my shoes together like a schoolboy getting a lecture from his teacher. Now, I ask you once more and I won't again. Will you accompany me back to Bar Harbor?"

"And if I say no?"

"If you say no, then you'll be traveling all the way back to Maine in the scruffy robe you're wearing." At her look of shock, he laughed. "That's right. I'll pick you up right off your feet and carry out to my car. And don't think anyone on the street will save you from abduction. This is the Big Apple, remember, not little Bar Harbor where everybody's business is everybody else's. Down here, no one wants to get involved."

"You wouldn't," she dared him, carefully placing her coffee mug on the counter, prepared to run away from him. This was a side of Adam she had never seen before, a side of him she didn't know how to deal with. Something in his voice warned her that he meant every word he had spoken.

"Oh, wouldn't I?" A glint shone in his eyes, a smile played around his lips.

"You're incredible!" Carly protested. "You have the effrontery to come in here and... and... threaten me!"

"And you had the effrontery to come into the restaurant and criticize my cooking! Seems as though we're two of a kind, Carly. Now hurry up and get your things together. And don't overdress. Jeans will do. I intend for us to take in a little sightseeing on our drive back."

"I will not! I have no intentions of going anywhere with you, Adam Noble, so you can get that idea right out of your foolish head." Carly crossed her arms over her chest and slowly tapped her foot on the worn tile floor.

In an elaborate gesture, Adam lifted his arm, pulled back the sleeve of his fine knit sport shirt and looked at his watch. "I'll give you three seconds to get to your room and dress. One...two..."

"No way!" Carly shouted. "There's no way you're going to come in here and give me orders! I'm a big girl now, Mr. Noble, or hadn't you noticed?" Her tone was snide, her lip was curled, her cheeks blazed with anger.

"Believe me, I've noticed, Carly." The softness of his tone was disarming, bringing further heat to her cheeks. "Shall we begin again?" he asked looking at his wrist watch. "One...two..."

"Ooh! You insufferable, egotistical..." Unable to control herself, she pushed him, nearly knocking him off his feet, leaving him swaying for balance against the apartment's small refrigerator.

Quicker than she would have thought possible, he regained his balance and flew after her, grasping her arm, pulling her backward, tumbling with her onto the carpeted floor of the living room.

"Adam! Let me go!" She struggled. "Let me go, right now!"

He pinned her beneath his weight, holding her arms over her head, looking down into her face, so close that she could feel his breath upon her cheek. Their gazes locked and held. Slowly the anger ebbed out of Carly's bones. Slowly, with each heart beat, anger was replaced with a yearning, a yearning to have his head bend to hers, to have his lips touch hers.

As Adam's eyes met hers, she felt herself falling into the depths of emotion, melting into him, allowing him to see her unmasked feelings, the desire for something outside herself.

As though in a dream, Adam's struggles ceased. His grip tightened, but this time it was with a strange brand of gentleness. Softly, his mouth claimed hers and his kiss deepened and became intense and swept her along with its persuasion.

Slowly, her arms circled his neck, her mouth yielded up to his and his tender, teasing touches. She heard him murmur her name against her ear, and when he lifted his head to look into her eyes, she could see desire ablaze there, a raw hunger that she knew was beyond her power to control.

"Adam!" she began to protest, but he misunderstood her cry for one of passion instead of one of protest.

His arms seized her, his lips found her throat, the V of her robe, the promising swell where her breasts began to rise.

He was wicked; he was tender; he excited her senses and commanded her pulses. She was his prisoner; he was her prey. She could not escape his loving, his strength. He kissed and caressed her, robbing her of her will, awakening in her a responsive fire that, unleashed, could consume them both.

Carly exerted weak protests against his chest, his arms, pushing, fighting to have him release her. Desire told her to surrender to his arms, his lips. Passion whispered and throbbed at his every touch, telling her that he alone could lead her to the heights of fulfillment and topple her into the realm of sensuality. Common sense pounded at the small portion of her reality that was not filled with Adam Noble.

"No...no...!" she begged, using the last of her strength to wriggle out from under him, knowing that if strength should fail, she would lose herself in the desire he aroused in her.

"Adam, no..."

Slowly, tenderly, he released her from his embrace. Patterns of emotions played about his face. His voice, when he spoke, was warm, husky, simmering with barely achieved control. "Carly." That was all, just her name. With a display of reluctance, he climbed to his feet and pulled her upright to stand in the circle of his arms. "Now, will you please get dressed and drive back to Bar Harbor with me? Tell me what airline; I'll cancel your reservation."

As though through a dream, she told him. Beneath his spell she was without a will of her own. She knew she would do as he asked. Do it and love doing it. Within, her heart sang. Of course she would drive back to Maine with Adam. Was there ever really any doubt?

Onward, onward, the road curved before them. Interstate 95 unfurled before them, dancing them through New York State, Connecticut, the few miles of Rhode Island and Massachusetts. At last, they left the Interstate for the more picturesque Route 1 just on the far side of Bath, Maine.

The day was still young, young enough for Carly to still feel the imprint of Adam's arms tight around her and the firebrand of his kiss on her lips. She wondered if the remembrance would ever leave her, to fade away like so many other memories. Somehow, she doubted it. She would mark this day as a milestone in her life. From now on it would always be "before the day that Adam kissed me," or "after the day in Jenny's apartment when Adam kissed me," or even "the same year that Adam made me feel like a woman."

The radio sang softly and Adam and Carly noted the bewitching names of the tiny hamlets through which they passed. Wicasset, Damariscotta, Friendship, old names, salty with the sea, foreign names reminiscent of farms and fertile fields.

And as they drove, they talked of many things. Mostly, Carly was content to lean back against the soft leather of the Corvette as the vehicle hugged the ground and whizzed them along and listen to the deep sounds of Adam's voice. He spoke of his deep love for his family, of his rambunctious brothers and keen-minded father, the judge. He told her of his love for this state of Maine and his concern for its people. One day, soon, she wouldn't be surprised to see his name on the ballot for State Senator.

With each sentence he spoke, Carly was imbued with an understanding of just how much family and citizenship meant to Adam. His eyes were toward the future, his feet planted very firmly in the present. In all truth, Melissa had been right about him. He was a man for tomorrow and beyond.

Her thoughts touched lightly on thoughts of Kyle. A man for the here and now. Somehow he could always make the most advantage of today and devil take the hindmost. Like his craft of architecture, Kyle built his life on accomplishments today—building for the present and looking forward to the next city and the next building. Roots were not a part of Kyle's vocabulary.

Roots. Generations. Dynasty. These were words with which Adam was fully familiar. They were the touchstones of his life and his reason for being. Building for the future. Security for his family, with always an eye to the world that family would inherit.

"We're coming into Rockland, Carly. What say we stop for a late lunch?" His voice broke into her thoughts.

"Umm. I'm starved."

"Well, I know just the remedy for that condition." Adam smiled. "I know where we can get the best hot dogs this side of Coney Island."

Carly laughed. "Don't tell me you have a penchant for hot dogs, not after all your bragging about being a gourmet cook!"

"Ouch! Well, the secret's out."

"Hot dogs it is. Now, don't tell me, let me guess. We're going down to the public landing, right? And there's this little old man with a heavy French accent who sells steaming hot franks and ice cold orange pop."

Adam laughed, the sound filling the interior of the automobile. "You've been here before."

"World traveler that I am, how could I not?"

Like a capricious breeze, the Corvette swung around the curves and descended steeply down a gravel track to the harbor on Penobscot Bay and to Pepe's hot dog stand.

The afternoon sun shone off the waters like a ransom in gold. The hot dogs were incredibly hot, the orange pop refreshingly cold and like two children with treasure, Adam and Carly absconded with the goods and walked the length of the public pier, munching and sipping.

In the distance, the outline of Vinalhaven Island could be discerned. The blue waters of the bay were salted with white sailing boats, their mainmasts seeming to scrape the sky, their brilliant sails creating a carnival of color.

"It's a little chunk of God's country, Carly. The water is so calm and peaceful, but we both know what it can be during a storm."

Carly nodded her agreement. "There are times I really don't know which I prefer, this calm or a good roiling storm. There's something about the power and force that excites me." Suddenly, Carly's cheeks pinkened. Wasn't that part of Adam's charm for her? His power, his force, and yet the appealing other side of him—his gentleness and tenderness.

"Funny how when people think of Maine they imagine windswept rocks and boiling sea beating surf against the beach. That's only true in the southernmost part of our state. The further north one goes, the shoreline becomes expansive bays dotted with islands where the trees reach down to the water and the land palisades into cliffs.''

''But there's no denying our twelve foot tides, Adam, when the shore can become a shelf of mudland....''

''Ah! But otherwise, who would be able to harvest clams and beachcomb...?''

''Do you always see an advantage to everything?'' Carly asked, a twinkle in her eye.

''Why not? I'm not exactly the cockeyed optimist, but there is usually something good about every situation. Take the house on Deer Island, for instance.''

As soon as he mentioned the island, Carly stiffened. She didn't want to go into a broad explanation of why the house seemed to be sold out from under him. Not here, not now.

Adam shrugged. ''If it wasn't meant to be, then it won't be. Besides, if I'm not missing my bet, it won't be long before Kyle finds his fancies going in other directions and the house might just be mine some day, after all.''

Carly sighed in relief. There was a lot of truth in what Adam said. ''Kyle told me he thought the house just perfect the way it is. I don't believe he's planning any major renovations."

"Kyle always did have an eye for perfection," he said, his voice closer to her ear than she had expected. She was startled, but not dismayed, to find herself wrapped in his tender embrace, his lips tracing a pattern from her ear to her cheek. He released her as quickly as he had embraced her and Carly felt bereft when he removed his arms.

"Look." He pointed to the water and to a sailing vessel tacking into port. "It's the *Victory Chimes,* the loveliest boat to sail these waters. She cruises the Maine coast and takes on passengers who work as her crew. I've always wanted to book passage but somehow I've never found the time."

"Oh, Adam, have you really? So have I! I've heard people talk about it and I fell in love with the idea."

"So have I," Adam agreed, a strangely intimate light in his eyes as he gazed at her. "I've fallen in love...with the idea." He pulled his gaze away from hers, gazing out to the horizon once again.

A heat spread through Carly, touching her breasts, her lips, her cheeks. Her heart beat a rapid tattoo, pounding, threatening to erupt from her chest. Was it possible, had Adam meant what she thought...? No, silly. You're reading into his words, she chastised herself. When Adam has something to say, he says it. Period. Besides, with the inimitable Simone Maddox waiting in the wings, she mustn't hope for more than a companionable ride back to the Harbor. A kiss was a kiss, it wasn't a commitment for life, she reminded herself. Yet, there was so much more. So much emotion and yearning... Don't, she warned. It was a kiss, not a promise. Period.

She was aware that Adam had taken her hand in his and was leading her back up the pier. He seemed mesmerized by the loveliness of the scene before him and was certainly in no hurry to go back to the sports car and make a hasty end to their journey. Bar Harbor was just a little over two hours away. They could have arrived well before evening, but Adam seemed disinclined.

Without asking if she was agreeable, he led her on a circuitous tour of the town. Behaving like tourists, they drove to the Ureneff Tuberous Begonia Garden where they marveled at the blossoms and plants and raced down the grassy slopes to where the sunken garden was displayed against an overwhelming natural setting of pines and birches and ferns.

They traveled to the Farnsworth Library and Art Museum for first-hand appreciation of the works of Andrew and James Wyeth. And finally on to the Farnsworth Homestead and its nineteenth-century Victorian mansion with its fabulous carriage house display of sleighs, wagons and smithy shop.

Their day in Rockland wouldn't be complete without a stop at the Shore Village Museum on Limerock Street where they viewed over a thousand artifacts relating to early Coast Guard and Lighthouse service history.

Through each exhibit, throughout the whole day, Adam kept Carly's hand in his complete possession. As she walked beside him, she was captivated by his easy, graceful walk and the sheer height of the man. With Adam beside her she felt protected from the world. And when she glanced up at him, it was always to find him smiling down at her, his eyes twinkling, his darkly handsome head framed against the scrubbed blue of the sky.

Each step was light and easy—painless, despite the amount of walking. She believed she could walk the world around if Adam were beside her.

With a pang of regret to have their idyllic afternoon come to an end, Carly settled back against the soft leather seat of the Corvette and watched

Adam take command of the machine. Before backing out of his parking space near the wharf, he turned to her, a long, searching light in his eyes. A gentle finger brushed a strand of hair away from her cheek, and although he remained silent, Carly felt his meaning. He was as pained to have the day come to an end as she was.

A few minutes later they were breezing along on Route 1 heading north. To home. Where everything was the same as it had always been and would always be. The real estate business, Melissa, Quincy...Simone Maddox and Adam's unavailability. Refusing to spoil the day by dwelling on the empty void that lay ahead, Carly began humming to the tune on the radio.

Adam's deep voice joined hers and they simultaneously broke into song. Their camaraderie was easy, the gentle part of friendship. It was difficult to believe that only this morning Adam's power had overwhelmed her, that he had ignored her protests and had wrestled her to the floor to hold her and kiss her and arouse a deep, sensual need in her that she had only suspected was there but which had never really surfaced before.

The late sun was shining in the window over Adam's left shoulder. She turned to look at him, his aristocratic profile outlined in gold. The dark hair near the nape of his neck cried for a trim, and it curled with a will of its own around his ears. Strong and firm, his jaw gave authority to his handsomeness, a masculinity that was definitive. His long legs stretched out casually before him as he worked the gas and clutch with ease. But it was his hands that she found herself gazing at time and again. Strong hands, capable hands. Flexible and well formed. The tiny hairs on his knuckles became golden in the light. Adam's hands that had held her, touched her, delicately yet with a demanding possession. Hands that could be gentle or arousing. Adam's hands that could trace delicate patterns of ecstasy or could quell a storm of anger.

"Bucksport is coming up. Hungry?" Adam's voice broke her out of her fascinations. "Should be dinner time by the time we arrive. Ready for an early supper?"

Carly laughed merrily. How easily Adam could slip in and out of local custom. Back in New York the term would have been dinner. Now only hours and miles away, he slipped into local jargon, referring to the evening meal as supper.

"Ever been to Jed Prouty's?"

"Once," Carly answered, remembering the quiet atmosphere of the old tavern with its romantic candlelight.

"Prouty's it is, then."

"Adam, no. Really, I'm hardly dressed for the occasion," she mourned, looking down at her jeans and tennis shoes.

"Both of us have suitcases in the trunk," he offered the remedy.

"And where will we change? In the restroom of the corner gas station?"

"I had something a little better than the gas station in mind." Before she knew it, he was angling the car off the road and pulling into the drive of the Jed Prouty Motel. Carly's eyes widened and her throat constricted, choking off her breath. Her heart plummeted to somewhere below her belt. How could he? After this wonderful, idyllic day. How could he? Her mind raced, her mouth refused to form the words, and before she could speak, Adam had stopped the car at the front office and hurried inside.

Sitting alone in the sports car, Carly wanted to bolt. To run. This wasn't what she wanted. If Adam thought that she was going to share a room, share his bed...disappointment welled within her. Despite the attraction between them, she was just not that kind of girl. Call it old-fashioned, call it prudery, even call it stupidity...he had no right to assume that she would gladly jump into his bed.

Suddenly, her hand was on the door latch. Then she swung her feet out and she was outside, outside and ready to run. The fresh breeze off the Penobscot River cooled her flaming cheeks, but there was little that could cool her rising anger. Her luggage. She'd be damned if she'd let him take off with her luggage. Her eyes fell on the ignition where the keys dangled. Hurriedly, she reached for them, searching through them for what she felt would be the key to the trunk. Hands shaking, she managed to fit the correct key into the lock. Her eyes fell on her bags and she struggled to lift them out of the cramped trunk quarters. Suddenly, she heard his voice behind her. "Let me help you, Carly."

She turned on him, ready for battle, and found him standing with a wide grin on his face. And in his hands were two sets of room keys.

"Both rooms face on the river," he informed her, seemingly oblivious to the turmoil his hasty stop into the motel had caused her.

"Both rooms?" she asked, wanting to be certain she understood.

"Doesn't that please you? I could change..."

"No, no," she breathed, smiling again, overjoyed that Adam had not assumed she would share his room. "The river is perfect."

"Let's get going then. I made reservations at the tavern for eight. That should give us time to prowl around and see a little bit of the town. What there is of it, anyway," he joked.

Joy soared in her heart and she silently cursed herself for having so little faith in Adam. Then her heart gave a little tug. Was it really consideration for her that had prompted Adam to obtain two rooms or was it because he really had no designs on her, that she didn't arouse in him the same feeling he excited in her?

Uncertainly, Carly followed Adam into the main lobby while a bellman carted their bags to the elevator. The bellman unlocked her room first and Adam followed him inside, checking to see that everything was to his satisfaction. He glanced inside the room, checking the lights and for clean towels. He picked up the bedside phone, checking for a dial tone and automatically snapped on the radio-TV to be certain all was in working order.

The uniformed bellman opened the drapes and turned on the air conditioner, instructing Carly as to its use. The nights were already growing quite cool even though it was only the end of summer, he explained, and showed her how to operate the heating unit.

Adam was at the door, checking the locks and the bolt, and seeing that all was satisfactory, he gave her a wink and told her he'd see her in an hour. "I'm right down the hall, Room 411. Call me when you're ready."

Exactly one hour later, freshly showered and coiffed, and wearing a soft silver-gray silk dress, Carly telephoned Adam's room. He answered almost immediately and the sound of his voice so close to her ear sent tingles down her spine.

One minute later, there was his knock on her door. Sweeping up her tiny purse, she stepped out of the doorway and right into Adam's arms.

His kiss was light, yet proprietorial, and Carly melted into the light of approval she saw there in his eyes. "You're a marvel, Carly. Always beautiful and always on time." There was a note of intimacy in his voice, a possessiveness in his touch, as he held her arm, leading her to the elevator.

"Do you like your room?"

"Oh, yes. The view of the river is magnificent. But not so spectacular as the view from..." she stopped herself.

"Deer Island," he finished for her.

Carly turned to him and looked up into his face which had become suddenly stony and intractable. He had told her that losing the house on Deer Island no longer upset him, but seeing the change in him this way, Carly knew better.

If she had expected her careless choice of words to throw a pall over the rest of their evening, she was wrong. Adam wasn't the kind of man who dwelled on disappointments. By the time he led her out to the car, he was laughing and joking with her once again.

"We have over an hour before our reservation," he told her. "If you'd rather, we can go across the road to the tavern and wait at the bar or we could take a spin through Bucksport and discover."

"Discover is the word of the day," she answered, liking the smile in his eyes when she agreed.

"I was talking to the bellman as he opened my room," Adam told her. "I pretended we were tourists and were totally unfamiliar with Maine. He told me about an old cemetery just down the road that's a favorite with visitors. Want to go?"

"Cemeteries aren't exactly my thing, but sure, why not?"

The engine purred its response to the starter, and within minutes they were parking on the road beside an area completely surrounded by a high iron fence behind which old tombstones rebuked their neglect.

"Anyone I should know buried here?" Carly asked as she followed Adam through the gates into the cemetery.

"No one we'd want to know, I'm sure. We're looking for the tombstone of Jonathan Buck, the town's founder. He was a judge who was prominent in the New England witch trials. It's believed that he condemned an innocent woman to the burning stake for lewdness and that his grave marker is indelibly stained with the imprint of a woman's leg."

"You're right. No one I'd like to know," she answered, peering at the worn inscriptions on the aged stones.

"Over here, Carly. I've found it!"

Carly stepped lightly across the clumps of grass and rocky ground to where Adam called her. There before her, was a tall, granite obelisk standing as straight as the day it had been installed. The face of it bore the name of Jonathan Buck, and on its gray exterior was the undeniable dark stain which looked remarkably like a woman's leg.

"Ooh, it's enough to give me the shivers. . . ." She shuddered. "How's that old song go? 'He Done Her Wrong!' "

"Or, 'Hell hath no fury. . .' "

Her attention was diverted and Adam stopped in midsentence. Off to the right, several feet away, lay a tombstone bearing the inscription, "Henry Schneider" and several feet away from that stood another, smaller and of unpolished stone, "His Wife."

Carly was unaccountably saddened and yet there was a spur of rage within her. Adam followed her gaze and instantly realized her feelings. Henry Schneider's stone bore dates of the early 1700's. It had been made of polished granite and, while of simple design, it was apparent that it had been made by a craftsman while the other stone was rough hewn and was crumbling from the effects of wind and weather.

Carly bent to touch Henry's stone. "Look here, Adam. Look at the dates. He was sixty years old when he died, and it's quite apparent that the stone was erected before his death. See how the first date denoting his birth and the hyphen following it are carved deeply and with a sharp wedge? The year of his death is clearly not as deeply inscribed and the numerals are larger."

Adam frowned, following Carly's train of thought perfectly. It wasn't unusual, when upon the death of someone in the family, to have a headstone erected for oneself, leaving blank only the date of death. Old Henry Schneider, it would seem, had buried his wife, erected the insignificant headstone for her, and purchased a much more elaborate one for himself.

"Oh, Adam, I feel so sad for her," Carly mourned, looking at the crumbling stone. "It doesn't even tell her name or the dates or anything. It only says, 'His Wife.' As though she had no identity beyond that. He didn't even have it read, 'His Good Wife.' Nothing. It might just as well have said, 'His Dog.'"

Adam hunkered down beside Carly, his fingertips gently tracing the lettering on the old gravemarker. "Poor Mrs. Schneider. We can only hope this isn't indicative of the life she led."

Suddenly, Adam bounded to his feet. Surprised, Carly watched him stride through the gates of the cemetery and out onto the highway, disappearing from her view.

"Adam? Adam? Where are you going?" she called after him.

"Out here, Carly. Come and help me!"

She followed the sound of his voice, puzzled at his sudden departure. When she found him, it was in the tall weeds at the side of the road where bright blooms of wildflowers grew. Adam was working with his pocket knife, gathering a bouquet of blossoms.

"Adam, you're wonderful!" she gasped, running to help him, holding out her arms for the bunches of flowers he handed her. Together they picked and chose, arranging a pretty bouquet for Mrs. Schneider's grave.

While Adam stood by, Carly placed the blossoms in front of the headstone, tenderly handling the fragile blooms. When she was finished, Adam reached down and plucked a flower from the many and tucked it into Carly's curls. "Mrs. Schneider would like you to have it," he told her, kissing her lightly on the tip of her nose.

As Adam walked her back to the car, Carly couldn't help thinking that Adam Noble's wife would never be an insignificant part of his life like poor Mrs. Schneider. Adam's wife would always come first in his life, not a possession. And he would expect his wife to take part in his life, to be his helpmate. Carly brought her musings up short. She wouldn't, she mustn't, ever think of herself in that role. Adam had done nothing, said nothing, to commit himself to her. And with Simone Maddox in the wings, he never would. Simone was the kind of woman who would be politically advantageous to have as a wife. Not she, Carly, who didn't know the latest fashionable labels to wear on her clothes or the newest, rising young artist. Simone had contacts and her family connections could help Adam in his political career. While Carly had only the vaguest knowledge of politics and her only dealings with the arts were the ones to get her office walls painted.

"Why so glum, Carly?" Adam asked and there it was again, that faintly intimate note when he spoke her name. It was as though he liked to say "Carly." As though her name came easily to him and rolled off his lips.

"Not so glum, Adam. I've just been reminding myself of a few truths."

"Not all women are like the unfortunate Mrs. Schneider, Carly." He touched her hand, squeezing it. "And all men aren't like old Henry, either. Take me, for example." He laughed, his eyes twinkling merrily. "I'd be certain to have the largest, grandest gravemarker ever erected for *my* wife!"

"You beast!" Carly shrieked, pummeling him on the arm as they entered the motel parking lot where they would walk across the road to the famous Jed Prouty Tavern. "Are you really so certain that you'd outlive your wife? Not planning on being a Bluebeard, are you?"

"Yup," he teased as they walked across the wide front porch of the old stagecoach run stopping place, "I fully intend to kill her with love."

He laughed when he said it but there was a serious note hiding behind his jocularity—something that set Carly's pulses racing, but she couldn't dwell on it to reason it out because Adam was showing her pictures and portraits of some of the famous guests who had once frequented the tavern. She gazed up into the stern visages of Presidents Van Buren and Stonewall Jackson and William Henry Harrison and John Tyler as Adam directed, but it was his face she wanted to look at, his eyes that held the mystery for her.

For a moment he turned to her and looked down at her and there was unspeakable tenderness in his voice. "I'm having a great time, Carly. I hope you are too."

Before she could answer that this was the most special time she had ever spent in her life, the hostess entered from the dining room and showed them to their table.

* * *

Upon leaving the old tavern after an excellent dinner of Maine lobster and prime rib, Adam glanced at his watch as they were crossing the parking lot to the motel. "It's after eleven. Not late by New York standards but certainly too close to the witching hour here in Maine."

Carly felt forlorn and bereft. She never wanted this night to end. She wanted their closeness and the magic to go on forever.

Outside her door Adam took her in his arms. She felt the beating of his heart against her own, and the breath seemed to leave her body. His embrace was warm, possessive, and his kiss was hot, mystical. She offered him her mouth, answering his demand, feeding his passion. When he at last released her, it was reluctantly because of voices down the hall. His eyes shone down upon her and she was tempted to reach up to brush a lock of dark hair from his brow. "Get a good night's sleep, Carly. Good night."

Hours later, after what seemed an interminable time falling asleep, the phone at her bedside table rang, jarring her awake. Groping for the receiver in the dark, her fingers made contact and she brought the phone to her ear. Adam's soft, intimate voice snapped her eyes open.

"Carly?"

"Umm?"

"I'm sorry, I shouldn't have wakened you, go back to sleep."

"Huh? No, Adam...what is it?" Why was Adam calling her? His voice didn't sound as though he'd slept. Was he having as much difficulty sleeping as she had had? Was it because he had lain awake thinking of her as she had of him? The tempo of her pulse quickened.

"Well..." he seemed hesitant. "I couldn't sleep. I decided to take a walk outside and I wandered out in back of the motel by the river. Go back to sleep, honey. I'm a jerk for waking you."

"No. You were walking by the river and what?"

"Hell. It's the trout! They're running!" His voice quickened and filled with a little boy's excitement that was contagious. "I asked the desk clerk about fishing gear and he kindly offered to lend us his. What do you say, Carly? What kind of angler are you?"

"Just give me two minutes and I'll be down in a flash!"

"Great! I'm at the check-in desk."

Carly bounced out of bed. If Adam wanted to share his adventure with her, she wasn't going to refuse. If Adam wanted to go fishing at...she glanced at her watch...three in the morning, then fish she would. Everything was wonderful with Adam Noble, everything...everything.

Jeans, an old pullover, a quick tug of the brush through her hair and she was ready to go. Remembering to pocket her room key, she pressed the button to the elevator, couldn't wait, and headed for the stairs, racing down them, blood pounding, running to Adam.

When she achieved the front desk, he caught her in his arms and swung her around, to the amusement of the desk clerk. "You're terrific, Carly. Come on, I've got everything."

Her tennis shoes were soundless on the tarmac surrounding the motel and made for easy footing on the steep, weakly lit incline that led down to the mud flat and the Penobscot River.

The water was inky black and faintly redolent of oil, but in the feeble light from the back of the building, iridescent flashes of color and light could be seen in the shallows.

"Shh!" Adam put his finger to his lips. "Trout are really skittish this time of year and any sound will spook them. Look at that, did you ever see so many? They've come in at the high tide to feed. Want to lay a bet as to who'll get the biggest?"

Devilment and competition spurred Carly. "And what's the prize?"

"Winner take all," Adam whispered.

Carly wasn't certain what she was getting herself into, but she nodded her head, agreeing.

"Come on, then. The clerk even gave me some bait. I'll bait your hook for you."

"Oh, no, you won't. My dad and I used to go fishing all the time. He said he wouldn't fish with a woman who was afraid of her own bait."

"A wise man, your father, a wise man."

Hunkering down, Adam and Carly prepared their hooks. Standing at the water's edge, they both cast in. Almost immediately, the bait was taken, the lines rushing out of the spools, the snap of fin and tail turning the water white.

Adam reeled his catch in easily, the trout's fury no match against his strength. He held it up, the light shimmering off its white belly. "You'll have to go some to best this one, it must be four pounds!"

"For your information, Mr. Noble," Carly grunted with exertion, "that's Moby Dick out there on the end of my line."

Her fish played out more line, forcing Carly to step into the inky water up past her ankles. Again and again she leaned backward, struggling to reel it in. Again and again the fish snapped at the end of the line, making Carly believe she would never be able to play it in. The lightweight rod bent almost in two when at last she had fought it into the water's edge.

"Whew!" Adam breathed with astonishment when he saw the size of the trout. "Well, the night's not over. Ready for another try?"

"You bet."

For the next several hours they followed the path of the feeding trout, walking down the mudflats farther and farther away from the motel. The bait was fresh, the fish eager and their harvest was bountiful.

Their excursion had taken them out onto a natural rock jetty where Adam declared himself the winner. The last trout he had reeled in was the granddaddy of them all, and Carly agreed to his win, too exhausted to continue.

Adam dropped down onto the rocks beside her, wiping the vestiges of water and bait from his hands onto his old jeans. Leaning back on his elbow, he surveyed the sky. "This is the second time we're seeing daybreak together, Carly."

There it was again, the way he said her name. His voice almost seemed to soften, its rich basso tones lighten, as though he were whispering an endearment. "If I remember correctly, we didn't see much of that sunrise, did we?"

Carly's nerves tingled as she remembered that first kiss. Every kiss with Adam seemed to be a first kiss, heady and intoxicating, filling her world, her senses.

Adam looked across the river to the sprinkling of far off islands glistening like jewels as the break of day illuminated them. It was almost as though she could read his thoughts. He was thinking about Deer Island and the Sinclaire house.

"Adam, about the Sinclaire house . . ."

"What about it?" His voice was casual enough but there was something beneath it, some bitter core.

"I really did try to contact you. Somehow, you never received any messages."

"Did you, Carly?"

"Don't you believe me? No, I can see you don't."

"What I can't believe is how I never received any messages. That home was my dream home, exactly the place I would want to live, raise children . . . I have no reason to believe . . ."

"That I really tried to get in touch with you," Carly interrupted, not allowing him to complete his sentence.

"No... I..."

Again she cut him off, rising to her feet, standing over him. "Yours is not the only integrity that can be offended, Mr. Noble! I, too, lay great store in my reputation and credibility!" Her voice was rising, broaching on a shriek.

"Carly, you don't understand...."

"Oh, I understand, all right. I understand that you think I'm a liar. That I double-dealt you. That I stole the house out right from under you and sold it to Kyle Dillon. Let me go, Adam." She shrugged out of his reach when he extended his arms to her. "I can't bear to be near you. No... no..."

He was moving in on her, following her across the rocks. He captured her, holding her tightly, abating her struggles to be set free. He gripped her head, holding it still for his kiss, his mouth moving over hers, demanding, hurting....

"Let me go!" she cried, pushing him away, taking advantage of his unsteady footing. "I don't want to see you again! Stay away from me. You offend me!"

"Carly, don't be silly. You never let me finish what I was saying...." There was hurt in his eyes but also a kind of arrogance too. As if she should push her feelings aside and believe whatever he had to say, as though he expected her to believe him.

"At least let me drive you home to Bar Harbor...."

"Forget it. I'll make it home on my own. I'll hitchhike, rent a car...a bicycle! Anything! And don't bother paying for my room. I'll pay for it myself...." Turning, she ran back to shore, each moment expecting Adam to catch up with her, to force her to be with him. Instead, Adam stood on the jetty, shoulders slumped, the fishing gear he would have to return to the desk clerk lying abandoned at his feet.

Later, after she was in her room, a tap sounded at the door. "Carly, it's me, Adam."

"Go away," she cried, choking back the tears. "I don't want to hear anything you have to say...why should you want to talk to a liar?"

"It's not that way, you never let me finish...."

"Go away, Mr. Noble, before I have to call the police and tell them you're harassing me. It might blot your burgeoning political career. Go away!"

There was a silence on the other side of the door.

Afraid to move, even afraid to cry for fear of being heard through the door, Carly buried her face in the pillow and choked back her tears and rage. Why? Why had he come to Jenny's apartment? Why had he given her an idyllic day, rife with romance, with tender touches and passion-filled kisses if he thought her a liar? Had he somehow expected her to foul up the deal for Kyle Dillon? Mess it up so Kyle wouldn't want the house so he, Adam, could have it? She was in the position to be uniquely useful to him in that capacity....

"No, no, no!" she sobbed, stifling the sound in her pillow.

Checkout was one o'clock and when Carly finally dried her tears and washed her face, it was after ten. She had to get moving. A quick call to the desk clerk informed her that a public bus stopped at the corner near the motel and traveled on to Bar Harbor. Her transportation home wouldn't be difficult. After writing down the time of the bus's arrival, Carly asked in a meek voice, "Has Mr. Noble checked out yet?"

"Yes, Miss, over an hour ago. He left a message for you at the desk, telling me I should give it to you. And, by the way, your bill has been paid...."

Carly didn't want to hear anything else and clicked the phone down into its receiver.

Chapter Eleven

Carly climbed down from the high bus step and waited for the driver to retrieve her luggage from the storage space under the vehicle. She glanced around expecting, yet fearing, that Adam Noble would drive up in his sporty car. When she saw that he wasn't anywhere around, she breathed a sigh of relief.

Things were going to be bad enough explaining to Melissa the delay of her arrival home. She should have been home by air shuttle yesterday. Now, here she was, arriving a day late and by bus.

Melissa could read Carly like a book and she would know in a minute that whatever the problem was her daughter hadn't solved it. Then she would cluck and hover the way mothers do when they're worried about their children.

The bus station was only a few blocks from the office and Carly staggered under the weight of her luggage with each step.

The little bell over the door rang as Carly entered the cool of the office. Melissa did all the motherly things Carly expected. She kissed her only daughter resoundingly and babbled nonstop for fifteen minutes. She went in the order of priorities. Quincy was off his feed; the microwave oven wasn't working and she was near to starving; the sump pump in the basement only works for you, Carly, and what did you do to it; the basement is flooded and why don't we eat out from now on.

Carly winced. "Mother, Quincy is off his feed because he's molting. The microwave isn't broken. I pulled the plug during the electrical storm we had before I left, and as long as there's peanut butter and jelly, you'll never starve. The sump pump only works if you turn it on." Sometimes, especially now, she felt as though she was the mother and Melissa was the daughter. She waited, hardly daring to breathe, for Melissa to continue.

"I'm glad you're back. Not that I couldn't handle things, but this office is so quiet without you. I was going to bring Quincy in, but I can't stand it when those green feathers fly all over."

It was like pulling teeth without novocaine. "How's business?" Carly asked bravely.

"Hectic. Terrible. Nothing is going right. The bank didn't approve the Simpsons' mortgage, the closing went off on the Brackett place with only a few minor problems, and the lawyer for the Ryans misplaced their escrow check and can't find it, so the closing was postponed till he does find it. Mrs. Ryan is in the hospital under sedation and her husband is threatening to sue everyone in sight. The Sinclaires are now making noises like they don't want to sell after all. Martha thinks they might have been just a bit hasty. Kyle Dillon is on the verge of a nervous breakdown. By the way, Carly, he called here several times. The messages are still on the machine. I spoke to him once myself. And," she said, her dark eyes twinkling merrily, "guess who else called you?"

Carly's heart thundered in her chest so loud, she thought for sure Melissa would hear it. Please let her say it was Adam Noble, she pleaded silently. He would have arrived in Bar Harbor early this morning.

"Well, aren't you going to guess?" Melissa chirped happily.

"Mother, I'm too old and too tired right now to play games. Just tell me who called."

"Adam Noble, that's who. He sounded upset. Can you imagine, can you even begin to imagine how I felt when I said I didn't know when you were coming home? Your very own mother not knowing. And then I had to tell Kyle Dillon the same thing. Carly," Melissa said taking a deep breath, "is Adam Noble the reason you went off like a scalded cat?"

"Mother, don't help, don't give me any advice, and above all, don't ask questions. Not now."

"Darling, you asked me how business was. I told you. Is it my fault things haven't been going right? I'm so worried about Quincy, Carly. Are you sure he shouldn't go to the vet? He's not even eating his licorice."

She had done it again. Every time Melissa stuck her foot in her mouth, she used Quincy to get it out. "You're probably right to be concerned, Mother. I think he should go to the vet."

"Good girl. You can take him. You are going home to take your bags aren't you? I'm going over to see Martha and try to make some sense out of this mess. She did say they were selling, and the agreement was signed properly by all parties. Kyle Dillon is within his rights to sue if he has a mind to. I'll see you later. By the way, how was New York?"

"Simply paradise, Mother."

"Good," Melissa said hastily. "See you... whenever."

Carly heaved a sigh of relief. Melissa was so...she made her tired was what she did. Fifteen minutes of her nonstop prattle was enough to make Carly long for earplugs and a safe haven somewhere in the wilds of Canada. If she could bottle her energy, she would make a fortune. Carly sighed again. She might as well go home to check on things and come back later in the day to catch up. Now that Melissa knew she was home she would be off for days at a time, leaving Carly to take care of things. Practicable, dependable, feet on the ground, Carly would see to things. She sniffed and brushed a tear from the corner of her eye. No more tears. That was a promise she had made to herself on the bus ride home. She would never cry over a man again. She would save her tears for something really important, like when Quincy was placed in a foster home.

The emerald bird met Carly at the back door, jabbering just as Melissa had done. Feathers of all sizes were floating everywhere.

"Hi, Quincy. This place is a dump because your feathers are making a mess. But as you can see, I'm back. Molting sure takes all the starch out of you. If you keep it up, you're going to be the skinniest bird around. Want some licorice?"

Quincy flew into his cage and settled himself on his perch carefully tucking his head into his wing. Poor thing, I should have his problems. Quickly, before the green bird could change his mind, she tossed the cover over the cage and then set about cleaning up the carpet of shamrock-colored feathers. The feathers in the trash, Carly plugged in the microwave oven and tested it. Perfect. Melissa could bake her TV dinners till the end of time. She flicked the switch at the top of the basement stairs and heard the sump pump roar to life. Her house in order, so to speak, Carly mounted the stairs to her room. She unpacked, taking her time as she unfolded each article and then hung it carefully on a scented hanger. She was disappointed when she finished. Only a half hour had gone by. Why and how had she become so conscious of time? She had never been a clock-watcher for that matter. It was depressing. Suddenly, she was a lot of things she had never been before.

Carly slumped down in the lavender slipper chair and massaged her temples. She shouldn't be tired but she was. Bone tired. Weary to her soul of this boring life she was leading. There had to be more, much more. There just had to be. Who was it that had said, "Life is what you make it"? Obviously, someone far more intelligent than she was. Or else that person had more guts than she did.

She was getting nowhere sitting here contemplating the state of what passed for her life. She had to get up, go to the office and make something happen. Ha! She slung her shoulder strap bag over her shoulder and drove back to the office.

Carly poured something that looked like a combination of instant cocoa and coffee into a cup and looked at it. She wondered vaguely how long Melissa had let it sit there and if it were two weeks old. She carefully set the cup down when she thought she saw something move in the thick liquid. She was sorting through the messages when the phone rang. Should she answer it or should she let the machine take the call? She hated to hear a phone go unanswered. "Hello," she said briskly. Silence. "Hello," she said a second time.

"Carly? This is Adam Noble. I was shocked to hear your voice, that's why I hesitated for a second. How are you, Carly?"

"I'm just fine...Mr. Noble." She wouldn't ask him how he was because she didn't care how he was.

Another silence. Ah, he picked up on the Mr. Noble. "I called earlier to see if you made it home all right. I left a message with your mother."

Carly smiled to herself. He had left a message. Amazing. "Really?"

"Are you telling me you didn't get my message?" Adam asked, annoyance creeping into his voice.

"No. You're the one who doesn't get messages. My mother told me you called."

"If you received my message, why didn't you return my call?"

"Mr. Noble, it might surprise you, but I have other clients who keep abreast of their business dealings and know what their priorities are. I do business my way. You handle yours any way you see fit. Actually, there was no reason for me to return your call."

There was a deep chuckle on the other end of the line. "You sound hostile, Miss Andrews. I thought we had made excellent progress the last time we were together."

Carly felt the devil imp perch itself on her shoulder. "Is that what you thought." It was a statement rather than a question. "Please get to the point."

"Do I have to have a point? Can't I just call you for the sake of calling? Just to chat and hear your voice?"

"Why don't you practice that line on someone else? You're taking up my time, Mr. Noble. What do you want?"

The amused voice that had turned to annoyance was now cold and brisk. "I want to hear from you why you sold the Sinclaire property to Kyle Dillon. I want to know what he promised you to steal it out from under me and I don't want any lies. Just a few simple facts, Miss Andrews."

"Of all the insufferable, arrogant...I don't have to listen to you. How dare you talk to me like that? I think you better clean up your act, Mr. Noble. When and if you do, call me, and if I feel like talking to you, I will and if I don't, I won't. And let me say now the latter is more likely than the former. Goodbye, Mr. Noble!" Carly slammed the phone back in the cradle so hard she thought it would crack. Immediately the white instrument shrilled. Seething inwardly, Carly flicked the switch to the answering machine to On and leaned back in her chair. Who did he think he was? How dare he address her in such a manner? Maybe Simone Maddox permitted it, but she, Carly didn't have to put up with it.

More angry than hurt, Carly closed the office. It would be just like wealthy Adam Noble to come storming into the office and strangle her. If she went home, she at least had a fighting chance. She had enough. She was a capable person. Hadn't she taken care of Melissa and Quincy after Dad died? And she had done it well. She wasn't flighty and irresponsible. She took her responsibilities seriously and acted on them to the best of her ability. She didn't like her business methods or her integrity questioned. She didn't like it and she wouldn't stand for it.

Carly careened into the driveway and was out of her car as soon as the engine was cut. She raced into the house and locked and then bolted the door.

Carly sat in the kitchen waiting for Adam Noble. She was so sure he would come to the house just to rail her again that she kept her eyes glued to the multipaned glass on the back door. An hour passed and then two. The coffee pot was empty and Quincy hadn't moved a feather. Carly snorted indignantly. Just when she thought she had the arrogant man figured out, he went and threw her a curve. She wished he would have come storming up the driveway spewing fire just so she could tell him he was trespassing and to get out of her life. She deserved the ecstasy of telling him what she thought of him to his face. She would live with the agony later. If she sat here much longer, she would take root. He wasn't coming and she better make up her mind to that fact. Whatever nebulous strand there was between them was broken. It was time to put romance out of her life and to get back to business. Determinedly, she began to count on her fingers the most important duties awaiting her. Suddenly it came to her. Kyle! She hadn't even played back the messages he had left for her. How could she have forgotten? "It's all your fault, Quincy," she snapped irritably. Again the green bird ignored her. "Men!"

Since the microwave oven was working, Carly tossed a potpie into a glass dish and set the timer. She ate it without tasting the cardboard crust and the semi-hard vegetables. Who cared if she died from frozen food? Time to adjourn into the living room and the boob tube. She sat with her eyes glued to the set, aware only of the vibrant colors moving before her.

Melissa came through the front door like the proverbial whirlwind. "I pulled your chestnut out of the fire. Carly, are you listening to me? Martha Sinclaire is over her attack of the jitters and the property is still up for sale. All we have to do is call Kyle Dillon and we're back in business. Carly! Did you hear a word I said? What's wrong with you? Did you cook anything for dinner? Did you take Quincy to the vet? How is the poor thing? Carly, when are you going to call Kyle Dillon? Do you want the man to have a nervous breakdown?"

Carly yawned. "Mother, I did not take Quincy to the vet. He's sleeping. No, I did not cook dinner, but I did steal one of your potpies and I even ate it. I will call Kyle Dillon first thing in the morning. And whatever in the world makes you think I'm not happy?" She stretched her lips into a grimace. "See, I'm happy. I'm also happy that Martha Sinclaire decided to sell after all. You're a born salesperson, or how about con person? What did you say to her to make her change her mind?"

"Dear child," Melissa said loftily, "I merely pointed out to her the error of her ways. Besides, anyone can sway Martha Sinclaire. She's a mother and she wants to be near her children. I'd do the same thing if you got married and moved away. When do you think you'll take the step, Carly?"

"Never from the looks of things," Carly retorted morosely. "A lot you care if I get married. All you want is to get rid of Quincy and have that stupid microwave oven to yourself. Well, I'm trenching in and you might as well make up your mind that you're stuck with me."

"Carly, I would give you such a beautiful wedding. With the commission from the Sinclaire property, you can even have a dowry."

"You're forgetting one thing, Mother. In order to get married there has to be a man on the scene. And I don't need a dowry."

"You're probably right. Dowries are passé now. You did leave me a potpie, didn't you?"

"If I'm not mistaken, I left you sixteen chicken, eleven turkey and seven beef pies. Take your pick or eat one of each. Don't forget to put them into a glass dish."

"I know how to use that oven, I'm not addlepated like you seem to think," Melissa said huffily.

"They're fattening," Carly said gleefully, aware that Melissa counted calories constantly.

* * *

Carly woke with the phone shrilling in her ear, demanding and insistent. "Hello," she muttered groggily.

"Carly? That you? It's me, Adam."

The sound of his voice reverberated through her like shock waves. The alarm on her nightside table stated that it was 5:17. Words refused to form in her throat.

"Carly," he began softly, "I remembered you like sunrises so I assumed you would be awake. You were, weren't you?" he challenged.

"Hardly," she croaked. "Look, Adam, if you're calling to upbraid me again about the Sinclaire property I don't want to hear it. Thank you for calling. Goodbye." The phone fell from her fingers and bull's-eyed into the cradle.

Carly fumed. The nerve of him to call at this hour and harass me. Tossing back the covers she swung her feet to the floor and stomped off to the bathroom. There was no sense trying to go back to sleep, she was too angry.

Twisting the water faucets on viciously, the shower raged, spewing steam into the room. Showering quickly and toweling dry, she quickly went to her closet and selected at random a sleek navy blue skirt. A tailored white shirt and her blue blazer would do for the day.

She sat at her vanity table and applied a scant amount of makeup that included blusher, mascara and lip gloss. A tug of the brush through her hair and she picked up her purse and was out the door.

Quincy greeted her with a loud squawk as she flew through the living room and out the back door to the garage. There was no way, no way on God's sweet earth that she was going to hang around the house and make herself available for any more of Adam's accusations.

The tires screeched as she made the turn at the corner. Bar Harbor was still sleeping. The streets were void of traffic, and milk bottles and newspapers sat untouched on front porches. Aside from Adam Noble, Carly felt as though she were the only person awake in the whole world.

Making a left onto Main Street, she automatically headed for the office. She was about to park when she realized that aside from her home, Adam would certainly try to contact her here. Again her foot pressed the accelerator and she sped off. Her route took her past the dock where the ferry stood sentinel. The ferry that had taken Adam and herself out to Deer Island.

There was the Fisherman where she had had dinner with Adam. The Coffee Shop, the marina, the park where the Nobles played their regular Sunday touch football game. Everything, everywhere, reminded her of places and times with Adam.

Tears blurred her vision as her circuitous route took her around the town. The Coffee Shop was still closed. By a glance at her watch it was only 6:07. Too early for business; too late for a future with Adam.

Swiftly, she pulled into a parking space in front of the office. If Adam wanted to track her down he would, whether or not she went to the office. She needed to be someplace that would put her on her own ground. Somewhere familiar, somewhere safe.

No sooner had Carly stepped out of her car and smoothed her skirt than she saw him, standing across the street, watching the office. Her first impulse was to jump back in the car and run, but it went against her grain. However much she didn't want to hear any more of his accusations, she was going to stand and face them. Then, she would turn on her heel like the lady she was, and walk away. Clean and simple. Once and for all.

She stood her ground, facing him, daring him to cross the street and approach her. Her dark eyes held a challenge, one that he couldn't refuse.

Adam stood, moving his long, lean frame from the side of the building. His dark hair glinted with blue lights in the early morning light. The sun was climbing the sky, lighting the town with its red-gold hues. The white boating denims he wore hugged his body, accentuating the trim length of his legs. A soft blue pullover that she knew, even from this distance, did wonderful things for his eyes, topped his slacks. He moved toward her, unhurried and determined. Almost like a cat stalking a bird.

As he drew nearer she saw the grim set of his face, the tightening of his jaw, the way his well-defined brows were drawn into a frown.

Her heart fluttered within her, her pulses raced and yet she stood, ready to do battle. He came nearer, near enough to touch. "You hung up on me Carly. I wanted to talk to you. I must talk to you."

Carly froze him with a forbidding look. Sticking to her resolve, she deliberately turned on her heel and walked away. Instantly, his arm shot out to grasp her. "Stand still. I have to talk to you."

Defensively, she pulled away, still walking, her back to him. He touched her again. "Carly..."

Without realizing it, Carly's footsteps quickened, still he was right behind her, reaching out for her. "Carly... I have to talk to you."

"No!" Carly shouted, "I've heard enough. You've said too much already." The last words were nearly a sob and like a child, she placed her hands over her ears and began to run. Places passed before her in a blur. Her feet pounded the pavement as she tried to escape. Why wouldn't he take no for an answer? Why must he pursue her this way? There was nothing she could say that would make him believe that she hadn't deliberately, for some unknown reason, engineered to sell the Sinclaire property to Kyle instead of to him. She had been insulted enough and she wasn't having any more of it.

Suddenly, a viselike grip closed around her arm, pulling her backward and right into his arms. "Now you *are* going to listen to me, and right now." As he held firmly to her arm with one hand he reached for her bag with the other. "I assume the keys to your office are in here," he said, hot anger in his tone. "I don't intend to let you get away from me until you've heard what I have to say."

Roughly, unalterably, he pulled her along the street back to the office. Resolutely, she followed. Protests were beyond her. She was helpless. There was nothing else to do but submit to him, listen to his accusations for one more time. Hopefully, it would be for the last time.

Digging through her bag, Adam came up with her keys. He tossed them at her. "Open it," he gestured to the locked office door. Obediently, she found the key and inserted it into the lock. Almost before she could withdraw the key, Adam pushed the door open and pulled her inside.

"Now you're going to sit there and listen to what I have to say," he said gruffly, pushing her into a chair.

"I don't want to listen to you. Every time you say something it's insulting. I've had enough, can't you see that?"

"Be quiet. Don't say a word until you've heard me out."

"No, I won't be quiet. If you have something to get off your chest, go tell it to someone who'll listen. Go tell it to Simone."

"What has Simone got to do with this? No, don't answer. Let me tell you. I don't know what you ever thought was between Simone and myself but let me tell you it just isn't so. Simone was here in Bar Harbor at the invitation of my father. Not mine."

"Very interesting. If it's true," Carly heard herself say, her anger matching Adam's.

"Of course it's true. Why would you think otherwise?" he demanded.

"Any fool could see the designs Simone drew on you."

"That's just it, Carly, they were her designs, not mine. As a matter of fact, she's not even here in the Harbor any longer. She left without a word to anyone while I was in New York."

For the first time Carly seemed to hear what Adam was saying and she was brought up short and found herself speechless. Simone was gone. Adam never had intentions of marrying her.... Suddenly she thought of a remark Kyle had made at the fish fry. "What girl wouldn't have designs on a man if she'd been seeing him for two years."

"What? Woman, where do you get your crazy ideas?"

Carly pulled herself to her feet despite Adam's glare and proximity. "From Kyle Dillon. At the fish fry he said he had met the two of you in Monte Carlo two years ago! That's where! And if you think I'm going to sit here another minute and talk about Simone..."

Adam grasped her shoulders, pulling her against him. She beat at his chest with small, tightly clasped fists. Her pummeling was ineffectual against his strength.

"I only happened to run into Simone two years ago in Monte Carlo. I've only seen her once or twice before she accepted the judge's invitation to Bar Harbor. Seems my dad thinks it's time I settled down and took a wife. And speaking of which, I've decided my father is right." His eyes burned into hers, making her already pounding heart beat faster. His hands came up and closed over the back of her head, lifting her hair, touching the delicate sensitive skin behind her ears. His mouth came crashing down on hers and she found she was incapable of movement, helpless against him. "I love you, Carly. I love you."

Carly couldn't believe her ears. Adam's voice was husky with emotion, and so close to her, close enough that she felt his breath upon her cheek. Again his lips found hers in a searing, passionate kiss that obliterated the world and demanded an answering response in her. When he drew away from her he looked down into her eyes. "I called you this morning because I *did* want to talk to you about the Sinclaire property. Now, now, let me finish. I started to tell you in Bucksport but you didn't give me a chance. I wanted to tell you that the house doesn't matter."

Carly heard her own indrawn breath. She waited, frozen with anticipation. "That's just a house," she heard Adam say. "I've already discovered that home is where the heart is, Carly, and you're my heart. Anywhere you are is my home. Marry me, Carly, tell me you love me."

Carly's mind was a whirlwind of confusion. He loved her. Even though he believed she had double-dealt him with the Sinclaire property. He loved her! She should be happy, she was happy, if only they didn't have this doubt between them.

"Say you will, Carly," Adam whispered, mistaking her silence for indecision.

Carly sank back against the desk, her hand falling on the buttons of her telephone answering machine. Suddenly, the sound of Kyle Dillon's voice filled the office, startling both Carly and Adam.

"Carly, I hate talking into these machines but I've no other choice. I'll make this quick. I'm going to South America. You won't believe this but I'm going to design a whole entire city! Me! Can you believe it? About that house. I'm afraid I'm not going to be able to buy it after all. I hate to disappoint the Sinclaires but there's nothing I can do about it. If I have to lose the deposit, so be it. Get me off the hook, Carly. From the look of things it's a five-year project. More to tell you. I'll call back."

Carly and Adam looked at each other in disbelief. The house, the Sinclaire house was available. Adam's dream house.

Deliberately, Adam leaned forward and pressed the button to listen to the next message. It was Kyle again.

"Carly, I know you always wanted Adam to have the house. So tell him it's his. I had a little heart-to-heart talk with Simone and after a few drinks she let it slip out how she detoured your telephone messages from Adam. It seems she wasn't looking forward to a quiet life in Maine, and you were too much competition. At any rate, after I put the fear of God in her and threatened to mention to Adam how a little scheming filly had duped him, it was easy to convince Simone to see the sights of South America with me. As for Adam, don't worry, Carly, he'll come around. In fact, I wouldn't mind a bit if you called your firstborn after me.... Wish me luck, Carly. Goodbye."

Kyle's message was so unexpected that Carly could only sit in her chair, thoroughly stunned by the news. Hesitantly she looked up into Adam's eyes expectantly. He was looking down at her, a strange light glowing in his eyes. His arms opened and she stepped into them, knowing she would never want to leave them.

"Carly, can you ever forgive me?" he whispered, the remorse etched clearly on his face. "What a fool I was. I believed Simone implicitly when she denied that you'd ever tried to get in touch with me. And then when Kyle... Can you ever forgive me? I should have known to trust my instincts. I kept telling myself that I should believe you but my pigheadedness kept getting in the way. All I knew was how much I wanted the Sinclaire house and..."

"Shh!" Carly intoned. She placed her fingers against his lips briefly, then slipped her arms about his waist. "I should have trusted my instincts too. I knew you weren't the kind of man to dangle two women on a string at the same time. Even when you explained about Simone..."

It was Adam's turn to hush Carly. But instead of touching a finger to her lips he silenced her with his own.

* * * * *